Joanie
Copyright © 2020 by Barbara Gale

All rights reserved. No part of this publication may be reproduced, distributed, or transmitted in any form or by any means, including photocopying, recording, or other electronic or mechanical methods, without the prior written permission of the author, except in the case of brief quotations embodied in critical reviews and certain other non-commercial uses permitted by copyright law.

Tellwell Talent
www.tellwell.ca

ISBN
978-0-2288-3337-6 (Paperback)

TABLE OF CONTENTS

Preface		vii
Chapter 1	Losses	1
Chapter 2	Adjustment	21
Chapter 3	Healing	29

for my mother, 'Joanie'

1927-2019

Preface

I always wanted to write about my mother's troubled childhood, even long after I moved thousands of miles away from her. Perhaps it was a way to remain close and to love that little girl who became orphaned at such a young age. My cousin once suggested that, because our mothers lost their own mother at such a young age, they looked to their only daughters for unconditional love. And that we somehow became our mothers' mother. It was a huge demand and we were constantly struggling to fulfill their need to be nurtured. Writing her story in her own voice helped me feel closer to her and to see the world through her eyes. Through the stories she had shared with me and my vivid imagination I came to know the grandparents I had never met. Finally it helped me appreciate the amazing strength my mother had to endure the challenges she did.

Mom's Story

Part 1

Losses

My mother died when I was five years old but I never knew the circumstances of her death until I was 17. By then I had reconnected with my younger sister Barb and was living in downtown Toronto with my Aunt Alice. Barb and I had decided to visit a well-known clairvoyant hoping to hear about the prospect of handsome beaus and happy futures but, as the three of us sat in the dimly lit room holding hands, the woman asked about our mother.

"What happened to your mother," she asked, eyes closed but faintly moving. I was surprised. Why bring up our mother? "She died when I was five," I whispered, watching her as she frowned. After a few moments of silence she said, "I see so much blood. Yes, I see your mother and I see so much blood."

That evening, when I returned to my aunt's house on Annette St., I demanded to know what happened to my mother. Why had no one ever told us? My aunt, a tall, stout woman with my father's dark brown eyes was putting cream away in the little fridge in the back pantry. She looked surprised by my questions and motioned for me to come and sit at the kitchen table.

"Joan," she said, sighing and taking a seat at the table with me. "Rilla, your mother, was a fascinating woman." She looked at me as though I didn't believe her. "She really was. She had so much energy and a real zest for life. But it was a hard life for her living way out there on that old farm where you were all born. No running water or electricity. Must have been at least two miles to the nearest neighbour." She paused. "But she never complained, even though it was a lot for her, looking after the three of you young ones, so close in age. And your dad, he was no help, always taking off on one of the horses and visiting one of the neighbouring farms." She chuckled. "He was a charmer, that brother of mine."

She looked at me, her dark brown eyes warm as if asking forgiveness for keeping it from us all of those years. "Now I can't say I rightly know just what happened to your mom, Joan. But this I do know. She was so happy when your dad got that job in Stratford. I remember the night they came and told me. She danced around this kitchen floor and said, 'Oh Alice. He is going to have a real job. A fine job. In an office where he will wear a suit and tie. And Alice, just wait until you see the house we bought. It is a splendid house. It even has a basement where I can set up my sewing machine.'"

"It was a big job, I recall, moving from the farm and all the way to Stratford. But your Uncle Wilfred helped them. And you kids were all quite excited about the move too."

"Well, a month or so went by and I never really heard from them. You see they didn't have a phone back then and you know how long the post takes. And then your dad called from a neighbour's phone one night. His voice was all broken up and I couldn't really understand him. He said your mom had died. He said that he found her in the basement and that she had died." She paused. "I can't ever remember hearing my brother cry before that."

Aunt Alice rose and went to pour a glass of milk. "Want some?" she asked. I shook my head. "But how"? I asked. "What happened?"

Aunt Alice took a sip of milk. "Well, your dad said he found her right on that basement floor." She hesitated. "And that there was lots of blood. And then the doctor came and examined her and he found, lo and behold, she was pregnant. "She looked at me. "It appeared that she tried to get rid of the baby, Joanie," (she hadn't called me Joanie for a long time). "You know that happened a lot back then. Women tried to abort their babies." She paused, "Well, I think that your mom was just so darn happy in that new house and with your dad having a steady job and all, well, she just didn't want anything to change that. Frankly," she said, "that's all I know."

I sat there on the hard wooden chair, frozen. Thinking of Mom and the blood and my father finding her there. How horrid.

Aunt Alice went on, "She looked so beautiful, I recall, when I saw her. Your dad bought a real nice coffin and put it right there in the living room of their new house. There she was in her finest dress. I remember it was dark green velvet, with this pretty lilac scarf she used to wear."

I suddenly had a recollection of it. I remembered the coffin in the living room. And I could see my dad bent over her as Donny, Barb and I stood beside him, dumbfounded. He was crying, "What am I going to do with you poor little buggers now?" I can't remember just how I felt except that I didn't like seeing him cry.

I sometimes try to remember how she looked and how she smelt. And I try to remember her touch and her voice. But it's all a blur. Either I was too young or I just tried to block it out. I don't know. Years later an aunt sent Barb and I a letter our mom had written to her when she was a teenager and engaged to my father. It was

Joanie

strange, thinking of her then as a young girl planning a country wedding. But what was mostly strange was to hear her voice in those words, to read the way she formulated thoughts, to have little recollection of a mom and suddenly she was alive in those words.

She was buried in a graveyard on the outskirts of Stratford. On Sundays after church Dad would take the three of us there. My older brother Don, who was seven at the time, took her loss the hardest. I recall standing by the graveside while he wept, clinging to the arm of my dad. Barb, only 3, stood there holding my hand tightly, unmoving, numb. I wanted to cry. I wanted to grieve, like my brother, realizing that she was a good mom and that she was not coming back from the ground. But I couldn't. I just stared at the spring-wet earth adorned with lilies. I couldn't feel anything. I felt only guilt in having no tears.

About a month after the burial Dad came home from work and called us all into the parlour. He was smiling. "I have some good news," he said as he sat in the armchair by the wood stove. Barb climbed up onto his lap and Don and I stood waiting. "I have hired a woman, a real nice woman to come and care for you." He paused putting his arm around Barb and drawing her close to him. "Now I know this won't be like a real mom. Nothing will ever replace your real mom for sure. But this woman is really nice. I just met her and I asked her lots of questions to make sure she was good enough to look after my kids." He said this boastfully. "She's young and she's pretty."

"But not as pretty as our mom," Don blurted out.

"Well, no," Dad sighed. "But she said she's a real good cook. And she can cook for us and wash our clothes…and,"

We all just stared at him wondering where he was going with all of this.

"Well, the truth is I can't afford to keep hiring babysitters to care for you while I'm at work. And Mary needs a place to stay. She just moved here from the East coast and is looking for any kind of work. It won't cost us so much as hiring babysitters." He paused and looked at Don. "It will mean, Donny, that you will have to move in with your sisters for now so Mary can have your room. At least until I build a room for you in the basement."

We didn't say anything and then Don burst into tears and ran from the room. I took my dad's hand. "It's ok Dad," I said, wanting to be a peacekeeper of sorts. Dad's face clouded over. He looked tired. "I don't know what else to do," his voice trailed off. And that is how we came to know Mary.

She was soft and pretty and her sky-blue eyes danced in the light of day. She brought sunshine into our troubled house. Soon after she moved in I fell off my new two-wheeled bike and ran into the house, tears streaming down my face. Mary immediately bent down, her long dark hair brushing my cheek, and kissed my bruised knee. "There, there," she said. "We'll just get a cold cloth for that and you come and sit with me until it feels better." I curled up in the armchair with her as she held the cloth softly on my knee and I nestled into the pure warmth of her. That's how it was with Mary. She was always happy and always there for us. Even brother Don came around and began to talk with her about a new friend he made at school or his growing interest in baseball.

Barb and I got brand new bunk beds and I got to sleep on the top bunk. Donny grudgingly moved into my little bed. After dinner Dad told us to get ready for bed while Mary cleared the plates from the table. "I'll come in to say goodnight," she encouraged us. So there we all three lay, covers pulled up tightly to our necks waiting for Mary. She'd tiptoe into the room and kiss each of us goodnight, smelling like summer lilacs and breath sweet as rain. Dad would come in some time later and if I was still awake he would whisper, "What's wrong Joanie? Can't sleep?" Truth was, sometimes I couldn't sleep. I'd lay awake for hours just thinking of things. Of Mom and why she had to die so young. And of Mary and whether she could be our mom.

A year or so after Mary moved in we were just finishing dinner when Dad announced that it was time for Donny to move into his own room. "Now Donny is almost nine years old it is time he had his own room," he said.

"But Dad," Donny said, "you haven't built that room in the basement yet."

"No, that's a fact," Dad admitted, "but Mary," he said as his eyes met hers, "is willing to move out of her room for you Donny."

"But where will Mary sleep?" Barb looked worried. Dad paused and said, evenly, "Well, Mary will sleep with me." I recall looking at Mary and seeing her bow her head, blushing as Dad reached over and placed his hand on hers.

And then the house became all sweetness and light. Mary's pretty eyes were brighter than ever and you could almost hear her heart beating as she gazed out the parlour window waiting for Dad to return from work. We watched for him too because he would often bring us a piece of liquorice or bubblegum. His presence in the house was electric, his tallness towering over us and his booming voice calling, "Well, what did all of you young ones do today?" He'd hug us each in turn, winking at Mary. And then, almost always he would go to her and touch her somewhere, a finger on her cheek or a hand on her elbow. She would look up at him and smile, glowing. And he would say, "I'm ravenous. Now what did our pretty Mary make us for dinner tonight?" Those were happy times, good memories to alleviate some of the sorrow and the grief over losing Mom.

I remember we had a neighbour, a Mrs. Hazel who lived by herself in the small bungalow next door. We would see her at times checking her mailbox or walking her little dog Daisy, around the block. She would nod and say hello. One day, a few years after Mary had moved in with us, Barb and I were walking home from school and she spoke to us, "Why hello girls," she said. "Are you just coming home from school now?"

"Yes, Mrs. Hazel," I answered politely while Barb knelt to pat Daisy.

"Well, my goodness," she said. "You are both growing up so much." I smiled at her. "And that brother of yours is going to be a tall handsome man like your dad, I reckon." We began to walk on but she continued talking. "But it must be crowded for you all in that little house. I recall there are only three bedrooms. Do you and your sister," (she directed this to me), "need to share that little bedroom with your brother?"

"Oh no," Barb interjected. "Donny has his own room."

Mrs. Hazel looked confused. "But then where does Mary sleep?" she asked.

Barb right away said, "Oh, she sleeps with our daddy".

That night over dinner Barb relayed the conversation. "Daddy we saw Mrs. Hazel today on our way home from school."

"Oh, is that so?" said Dad, helping himself to more scalloped potatoes. "And was her little dog, Daisy, with her?"

"Yes," said Barb. "And she asked where Donny slept and where Mary slept."

"What did you say?" Dad asked evenly.

"Why, I told her that Mary slept with you Daddy." Everything became quiet for a moment. And then Dad rose from the table abruptly, pushing his chair back so that it frightened me. Mary bowed her head and was really quiet. I had these knots in my stomach feeling like something was wrong but was not sure what it was.

Things began to change after that. My dad became more irritable and we didn't anticipate him coming home from work the way we used to. And Mary became melancholy, going about her tasks in a methodical way. Still, I was beginning to learn about the ways of love and I could see without a doubt that she loved him. Her eyes lit up when he entered the room and she hung on his every word.

One day I came home from school and called for Mary. I wanted to tell her that I had done well on a math quiz. "Mary," I shouted as I ran around looking for her,

Joanie

wanting things to be more like they used to be. But she wasn't in the parlour, nor the kitchen. I went up to her room, the one she shared with Dad and found the curtains closed and clothes strewn around the room. Mary was sitting on the bed, quietly crying. She didn't see me and I didn't know what to say or what to do so I just left. But my heart ached for her.

Later that evening Dad came into our room as we were waiting for Mary to come and say goodnight. "Tomorrow we are going to have a visitor come for dinner," he said quietly. We rarely had visitors so waited for what he would say. "I have invited Isobel, my secretary at the office, to come over." He looked at each of us in turn. "She is a very nice woman. You will like her." None of us said a word. "And kids," he added, "I don't want you to talk about Mary and where Mary sleeps to Isobel. That is family business."

Isobel came over the following night, bringing us all little gifts. I remember mine was a bright red yo-yo. I hadn't had one before and was delighted with it. And then the strangest thing happened. Mary called us in for dinner but she didn't join us. Without a word she brought all of the food in, lay it on the table and went up to her room. It was really quiet and I missed having Mary with us. I wondered if I should go and see her but didn't think my dad would like it if I did. We all three sat quite solemn as Isobel and my dad talked about their work at the insurance agency. Later, Mary came back downstairs and cleared the dishes from the table.

"Now Joan and Barb," my dad turned to us. "You help Mary clear the dishes away." We right away jumped up, relieved to leave the table and to help Mary.

Isobel began to come over quite a lot after that. And sometimes Dad said he would be home late because he was spending the evening with her. She was nice enough, always bringing us candy or a little gift, but I could not really say that I liked her. She wore fancy dresses with high-heeled shoes and bright red lipstick. When she bent to kiss us we had to wipe smudges of red off our cheeks. Dad would laugh at Barb and I, "Now what's wrong with a little lipstick on your cheeks, girls? You'll be plastering it all over yourselves one day." Still, when Isobel was at the house there was a formality that we weren't used to. Mary would retreat to her room during dinner and Isobel would try to make conversation with us. But it was a wounded house, and we three didn't much feel like talking.

One September, soon after we began our new grades at school and only a few days before my ninth birthday we returned home from school to find Mary pacing the kitchen floor, wringing her hands. You could see she had been crying. "It's your dad," she said. "He's in the hospital."

We all three stood there, frozen. And then, sweet Mary, forgetting about herself and worried what this would all mean to us, bent to comfort us. "It will be ok, kids. Don't worry. Maybe we can go and see him at the hospital after we have a bite."

That evening when I saw my dad lying there in that hospital bed my heart stood still. He didn't look like our dad at all. His eyes were vacant and his skin greyish. Isobel sat beside him and looked at us blankly. "Shortly after he came into the office this morning he began vomiting blood," she said quietly. "I brought him in here and they are doing some tests."

Dad winked at us, his way of telling us not to worry. But I was frightened. I didn't like seeing him like this. He looked so weak and his breathing was shallow. This wasn't him, not our strong handsome dad. "We won't stay too long," Mary whispered as we all stood around not really knowing what to say or do. When a nurse came in Mary suggested we leave and I recall, as she leaned over to say goodbye to him, his large brown eyes looking up at her so tenderly.

Dad never made it out of the hospital. The tests determined the source of the bleeding was from a peptic ulcer and the doctor decided to keep him in the hospital to keep an eye on it. Every day after school Donny would walk Barb and I the seven blocks to the hospital to visit him. On Saturdays and Sunday afternoons Mary would accompany us, bringing him one of his favourite pastries or some candy. Those days normally found Isobel sitting faithfully by his bedside. I remember that, because when Isobel was there, Mary barely spoke a word.

One day after school we walked over and saw Mary in the room alone with Dad. They didn't hear us as we stood in the doorway and witnessed the intimacy of her lying against his chest weeping as he gently stroked her hair. "Please dear," he said ever so gently. "Try not to cry. It will be okay." His voice became husky and I saw tears well up in his eyes. He gazed down at her. "This wasn't much of a life for you anyway," he paused. "I am sorry Mary. I am so sorry, my darling." He cleared his throat. "I wish I could have given you more."

A few days later we found Isobel and Mary both with him and there was a solemnity in the air. I remember Dad looking so tired and weak that day. But he smiled at us. "Well, kids," he said. "I guess we need to make some plans."

"What do you mean?" Donny asked
, wide-eyed, looking frightened.

"Well," Dad continued. "The doctor said that I may not get better. He said that they can't control the bleeding and they feel surgery would be too risky." He looked at each of us in turn.

Joanie

Barb threw her arms around his neck and cried, "No, no! You have to get better dad!" He put his arm around her and drew her close. I stood by in shock feeling nothing really. But I had recollections of standing around my mother's coffin feeling similarly dazed and numb.

Donny frowned, looking scared said, "But, why?"

Reaching for Donny's hand and speaking slowly, faltering between breaths, Dad said, "Well, I can't really answer why this is happening, son. I don't know why I got sick like this. And I know it doesn't seem fair that you first lost your mother and now I have to get sick" He stuttered. "I am trying to make some kind of sense of it. I have been praying for some answers but" his voice trailed off, "I just don't know."

As Dad was talking Isobel sat on the chair by the bed, motionless. It was Mary who reached out for me, standing so alone there. She put her arm around me and drew me close. "It's okay to cry Joanie." She hugged me. "Just cry." But I couldn't. I could only stand there, immobile.

All was quiet for a moment. Then Dad continued speaking between shallow breaths, "And so, kids. I have been talking with some of the family. I need to know that you will all be okay," he cleared his throat, "in case I don't get better." He looked at Donny first. "Donny, Uncle Roy has agreed that you could live with them. His boys, Bus and Roy Junior would be happy to have you there as well. So, I think this will be a good place for you." After some time he turned to me, I guess because I was the next oldest. "And Joan, Joanie, come here sweetie," (I don't think he had ever called me that). "You are going to go to Aunt Pearl's house in Galt. Her Barbara is close to your age so she will be some company for you." He held my hand and looked at me with those deep brown eyes. "Now Aunt Pearl is different from your mom." He paused. "And different from 'our' Mary'" He smiled at her. "I mean she is strict. She likes to keep the house real clean and all." He paused and rested a moment. "But I think it will be a good choice for you." And then, he looked down at Barb who couldn't stop crying. "Barb," he lifted her face and taking his handkerchief from the nearby night table began drying her tears. "Aunt Alice said you could go and live with them in the city." His voice broke. "I think you will like it there." And, that was that. Our futures decided. Divided. Dad coughed and took a sip of water. He looked very tired and Mary motioned for us to leave.

Walking back to the house we all in turn clung to Mary. "But Mary," Donny sobbed, "Why can't you look after us?"

"Yes, please, please Mary, can't we live with you?" Barb pleaded. I thought as well that this would be the best of an already horrible situation and waited for what she would say. After all, didn't she love us? Didn't she want

Joanie

us? She acted like she did. Besides I was trying to get my head around the chance of Dad not being there for us which was already an impossible thought. How could we say goodbye to our Mary as well?

With tears in her eyes she quietly said, "No my darlings. I can't look after you. I will have no money, no place to live. The house needs to be sold and the family has agreed to care for you." She hesitated. "And I need to move on." We were home by now and she opened the front door. "Much as I would love to stay right here, right in this house with you, I can't. I just can't."

I marvelled at Mary and how she changed with the decline in my dad's health. It was like a bird took her spirit and flew away with it. She was like a shell of her former self, quietly going about her chores. Once I found her weeping in her room. I couldn't bear to see her unhappiness. I went over to her and put my arms around her. "Mary, I think my dad loves you, not Isobel." I had this desire to reassure her of what I believed to be true. She hugged me tight that day. I think she liked what I said. I felt kind of grown up.

She left soon after that. She said she was going back to her parents' in New Brunswick. She didn't wait to see what would happen with dad. Its like she knew he wouldn't make it. Aunt Alice came up from the city and took the three of us to the train to see her off. Our pretty young Mary all dressed in a dark grey suit with a brimmed hat. The light had gone from her eyes but she still had that warm inviting smile and she did her best to reassure us. "Now, listen all of you," she bent down to speak with us. "I want you to write to me and I promise I will write back." She smiled. "I'll tell you all about the ocean and my walks on the beach. The Bay of Fundy is a lovely place, you know, and when you get older you can come and visit me there." And then, the whistle of the train that took her away. Took our Mary away from us. Such a mournful, haunting sound and whenever I hear it, I think of her.

I can't remember the last time I saw Dad because later that day Aunt Pearl came to take me with her to Galt. Donny, a tall boy of 14 now, hugged me goodbye and told me to be good. Barb put her arms around me and cried, "Joanie I don't want to go and live with Aunt Alice." I just stood and looked at her blankly. What could I say? This was our life now and there was nothing any of us could do about it. I hugged her and looked away. Aunt Pearl was waiting impatiently. I don't know what ever happened with the money from selling the house or whether it was given to our relatives for our upkeep. No one ever told us.

Two weeks later I was carrying a bowl of cereal across the kitchen floor when Aunt Pearl walked into the kitchen and bluntly said, "Your dad died last night." Just like that. No hugs, no stories of his last days or his dying words. Just that. I dropped the bowl and it crashed on the tile floor.

Joanie

I still hear the sound of glass breaking on ceramic when I think of that day.

It was a grey and melancholy day when we put Dad to rest. Clouds hung low and a fine misty rain drizzled methodically. We all stood under our umbrellas as Dad's brothers, father and a handful of friends lowered him into the ground. I held tightly on to Barb's hand as she wailed mournfully. Donny stood by us as a protective older brother with one hand on each of our shoulders. There was a huge hole in my heart.

Part 2

Adjustment

I shared a room with my 10-year old cousin Barbara, in the small bungalow Aunt Pearl and Uncle Al had in Galt. Barbara, who was their only child, had an air of self-importance. She tossed her curly dark hair around frivolously, suggesting how pretty it was compared to my straight mousy brown locks. The house was on a quiet street where every house looked the same, red brick bungalows with hedges bordering their front lawns and gardens running alongside the front of the houses. Oak floors ran throughout the house except for the paisley linoleum that brightened the kitchen. Breakfasts and lunches on the weekends were informal, unstructured events but Aunt Pearl made sure we all sat around the table for dinners. "We need to have at least one meal a day where we eat together as a family," she would say.

On school days I was expected to do homework immediately following school and Aunt Pearl would check it before I was allowed to have any free time. Barbara's chore (she right away instructed me to call her 'Barbara' not 'Barb') was to set the table for dinner while mine was to clear the table and wash and dry the dinner dishes. At 8 pm I was expected to be in bed with the lights out. Barbara, because she was all of 6 months older than me, was allowed to stay up until 9.

To be honest I was glad to have that hour to myself in bed. I did not much care for Barbara and I had the feeling she didn't like me at all. Or maybe she just didn't like the fact that I was living there. She would coldly tell me not to touch her things and she never walked with me to school or introduced me to any of her friends. Maybe she was ashamed of me, or embarrassed by me. She had a way of getting whatever she wanted from her mom and dad, acting sweet and innocent to them but then like another person when we were alone together.

I learned about loneliness that year in Galt. I had little energy to invest in making new friends at school and felt despised by my cousin and scrutinized by my aunt at home. I escaped into novels, dark stories meant for older children, such as 'Ethan Brown' and 'Wuthering

Heights'. At night, if my chores were done I would find a quiet corner of the house and read until it was time for bed. I loved envisioning myself the beautiful Catherine on the English moors or the young Mattie caring for Ethan's wife, Zeena. And then I would lie in bed and imagine happier times with Mary, my dad, Donny and Barb. I would try to remember times with Mom and could recollect sitting on her lap while she read to me but not much beyond that. I didn't cry much, still feeling more of a numbness about everything than a grief, but sometimes I would have this reoccurring dream and wake with tears running down my face. I couldn't remember much about the dream except there was an old farmhouse and this long dining room table all set for dinner. But everyone had left. There was no one there. And I woke in horror because of this abandonment.

I felt so lonely as Christmas approached remembering happier Christmases in Stratford. Dad would come home from shopping with a twinkle in his eye and tell us all to stay in the kitchen and we knew he was hiding the gifts he had for us. I remember one year he took us into a pretty pine forest down by the Avon River where we cut our Christmas tree.

"Now I don't rightly know that we can do this here. Not when they are trying to sell these trees in the store," he said. "But, this is the way I grew up. We always cut our own."

And then we stood around while he cut the tree down and urged us to sing, 'Oh, Christmas tree'. Mary made these delightful little Christmas shortbreads called Swedish dainties that had a cherry plopped right in the middle of them and we played Christmas songs on the old phonograph and had cookies and hot chocolate as we decorated the tree.

Christmas morning arrived that year at Aunt Pearl's house in spite of my trepidation and Barbara insisted we get up early because she couldn't wait to open her gifts.

"Merry Christmas Mom and Dad," she said opening the door to their bedroom. But Aunt Pearl was already up and in the kitchen making coffee for her and Uncle Al. We gathered around the tree and Barbara opened all of her gifts. There were a few for Aunt Pearl and Uncle Al as well. But there were no gifts for me that year. Nothing. I didn't really care because the only things I really wished for were impossible to have back. But it felt awkward sitting there while they all opened gifts as a family.

A few months after Christmas Aunt Pearl called me into the kitchen and said she wanted to talk with me. "Come and sit down for a moment, Joan," she said. Her greying hair was tied back tightly into a knot and she was kneading bread on the kitchen counter. She turned to look at me with those same dark brown eyes that were my dad's, "Well Joan," she said, turning back to the bread. "Barbara seems to think that you are not very happy here." She turned to look at me. I bowed my head, not knowing what to say. "And so she thinks that maybe you would be better off living somewhere else." It felt like spiders were crawling inside my stomach. Who was Barbara to say what I wanted, what I needed? I waited for what would come next. "Now, I know that I told your dad, my dear brother, that I would care for you to the best of my ability. And I know he wanted to see all of you nicely settled before he…" Her voice trailed off. "So I feel like I am going back on my word to even think of you leaving." She sighed. "But if what Barbara says is true and you are not happy here then maybe you should live somewhere else." She looked at me. "So I am asking you, Joan. Are you happy here?"

I squirmed on the hard kitchen chair and a tear rolled down my cheek. "I miss my dad, " I whispered.

"Now, now," Aunt Pearl continued. "There's no use crying about that. You know he isn't coming back. So we have to figure out what is best for you now." She divided the dough into two balls and placed both to rise on the counter in the sun. "Anyway I talked to your Aunt Lottie. She has no children you know. And I think she would enjoy having a young girl such as yourself around." She paused. "She said it would be fine for you to live with her and uncle Jim in Woodstock. Now, I've thought about it and I think your dad would approve." And then, in a curt, matter of fact way she added, "I have done my part anyway."

I lived with Aunt Lottie and Uncle Jim in their small house in Woodstock for two years. It was a lonely life there and I spent most of my free time alone with my thoughts and my books. Every evening the three of us would sit by the wood stove in the living room while Uncle Jim read aloud from the bible. And then I would escape to my room to have a quiet hour of reading before Aunt Lottie poked her head in the door and said, "Lights out. Goodnight Joan."

I became used to a quiet life and my grief settled into a complacency of sorts. I saw Don and Barb only at Christmas when we gathered at one of my aunt's houses but I wrote to them and to Mary faithfully every week. I looked forward to seeing what the post would bring and, if there was a letter for me from one of them, I found a quiet corner in the house to devour every word. Mary talked about the new family she lived with and how she was busy being a nanny to twin 6-year -old boys. Donny spoke positively about settling in well with Uncle Roy, Aunt Vera and their two sons who lived in a small town a few hours east of Toronto. It was Barb that I worried about. She wrote despondent, lengthy letters expressing feelings of not fitting in with Aunt Alice's large family and feeling lonely all the time. I thought I would grow up with Aunt Lottie, at least live there until I finished school and could get a job of my own. Then I dreamed of moving into the city to be closer to Barb. So I was surprised one day when Aunt Lottie informed me that was not to be the case.

"Yes, by golly," she said, gently touching her stomach. "I didn't think I could conceive a child. But," she paused and threw her hands in the air. "Thank the Lord. I'm going to have a baby!" She was sitting on the armchair by the fireplace as she told me this and her face, slightly flushed, radiated with a childish excitement. And then Uncle Jim came into the room and put his hand on my shoulder in a kindly manner. Aunt Lottie smiled at him and then looked back to me. "Now Joan," she said, "I'm afraid we will need to fix up your room for the baby." She cleared her throat and paused a moment. "So Uncle Jim and I have talked." She paused and looked away from me. "Well, you know Grandpa and Grandma are getting older and could use some help on the farm. So," she hesitated. "We thought it might be a good idea for you to go up there and live with them."

I was stunned. I never saw this coming. I braced myself, "Couldn't I live with Barb?" I whispered.

"No, Joan, you know there are seven children in that house now including your sister. There is simply not room for you there. Besides," she reminded me. "You are 12 years old now and could be a good help to your Grandma and Grandpa. I have talked with them and they said they would be happy to have you there. She rose from the armchair. "So, it has been decided. We can drive up next weekend."

Part 3

Healing

1

You leave the highway and drive along a winding gravel road to get to the little town of Coldwater. It borders Canadian Shield country, laced with pretty pine forests and rock. I gazed out the window as we drove away from my life in Woodstock and tried to feel some optimism about what was to come, remembering the beauty of the countryside there and happy times when Dad was with us. I thought back to the last time we all went up there as a family. It was a hot July afternoon and Dad suggested Barb and I walk back the lane with him. "Come on girls," he smiled, squinting in the bright sunlight. "I have something to show you." We followed him back through the field, once used for cattle, and climbed a barbed fence into a forest. Not long into the forest we reached a clearing and Dad led us to a towering maple tree. "See girls," he said, tracing his finger along initials carved into the tree. "G.S. and R.C. Your mom and I did this soon after we became engaged. We used to come here sometimes." I gazed at the inscription, imagining their love back then and envisioning them, like Catherine and Heathcliff, wandering back the lane and declaring their feelings for one another. Perhaps my wild imagination and thinking of Dad growing up there would help me settle into this new life.

We pulled into the long driveway and I saw the old brick farmhouse to be sadly in need of repair. Paint was peeling off the trim and the roof was sagging over the woodshed that had been tacked onto the house some years ago. Still, it was September and a lovely day. The sun beamed over the house, in spite of its state, and purple and pink cosmos grew wildly where there had once been a vegetable garden.

"Ah, food for the soul," I thought to myself, smiling inside. Aunt Lottie turned to me in the back seat.

"Well, here we are Joan."

I could see Grandpa watching for us from the kitchen window and then Grandma came out onto the back porch. She had aged in the last three years. Her grey hair was tied back, the odd strand brushing over her pronounced cheekbones. She walked with a cane now, her body stooped slightly and her steps slow and methodical. I knew she had seen better times remembering a photo Dad had of her dressed finely in a strapless dress and pearls. She had been a beauty in her younger years. Still she took my hand gently and looked at me with those same beautiful brown eyes. Dad's eyes. They were bright in the anticipation of our arrival and I suddenly felt happy.

"Joan," she said warmly. I hugged her tight. I hadn't seen her since Dad's funeral. My heart was in my throat and I felt like crying.

"Come in," she smiled and kissed Aunt Lottie and Uncle Jim. "Dad is waiting."

The woodshed, which served as a mudroom as well, was cluttered with firewood, bags of chicken feed, woollen overcoats and rubber boots. Here we removed our jackets and hung them on the few available hooks. Entering the kitchen I saw Grandpa slowly stand from his rocking chair by the window. His tallness, so like Dad's, was impressive as he reached out and took each of our hands in turn. "Well, well," he said with a smile, "good to see you all."

The familiar old oak table still stood in the middle of the kitchen, brightened with a flowered tablecloth Grandma had put on in anticipation of company. It was nicely set for tea with china that had been in the family for some time. A wood fire crackling in the Findlay oval cook stove brightened and warmed the room. However, in spite of the fineness of the setting I couldn't help but see that the wallpaper was peeling off the walls in places and the wainscoting was in need of a fresh coat of paint.

"I've some fresh blueberry scones," Grandma smiled, carrying a plate over from the sideboard. We settled around the table and Aunt Lottie talked excitedly about the baby. "I wonder if we'll be parents by Christmas this year," she said, her face flushed. "If so, you may all want to come up to Woodstock to see us."

Grandpa nodded reaching for a second scone. "Well, we'll see about that dear. The old Plymouth isn't running too well and the train is getting more and more costly."

"How long can you stay?" Grandma asked, looking to Uncle Jim.

Uncle Jim reached for Aunt Lottie's hand. "Only till tomorrow," he said.

Following tea I cleared the dishes away, eager to explore and to be alone with my thoughts. "Can I help wash the dishes, Grandma?" I asked.

Grandma turned to me, "Yes dear. But you first need to fill that old kettle in the back kitchen with water from the pump there and put it on the wood stove to heat. And then, why not take your things upstairs to the little room I have fixed for you?"

The back kitchen was a pantry of sorts. Lining one wall were shelves stocked with Grandma's preserves: blueberry jam, maple syrup, canned tomatoes and stewed rhubarb. I found the kettle on a sideboard where there were crocks of flour, sugar, rice and oats. Filling the kettle from the hand pump that emptied into the sink I peered out the window to the garden of colourful cosmos. I wondered if Grandma would let me pick some for the table.

And then, taking my suitcase, I went into the parlour, which was sparsely furnished with a wine red couch, two wooden rockers, standing candelabras and an old pump organ. I was suddenly grateful for Aunt Lottie insisting I take piano lessons, remembering happier times when Dad pumped away familiar carols or church hymns. Perhaps I could brighten some of my grandparents' evenings with some of the hymns I had learned to play.

The stairs creaked as I mounted them and I heard strange noises coming from above. I was surprised to open the room at the top of the stairs to see several chickens strutting around pecking away at grains and seeds. I curled my nose up to the foul smell and glanced around the room. Willow roosts were nailed between the walls and a tarp hung over a door of sorts that allowed them access to the outside. I hadn't remembered this from previous visits. Later Grandpa told me that the chicken house was in such need of repair he thought why not put them in one of the empty room upstairs? "Besides," he added. "Why heat two buildings when they are quite happy up there?" He proudly showed me a ramp he built that ran from the tarped window to the ground and routinely at daybreak and dusk there was the sound of a flurry of chickens mounting and dismounting the ramp.

I opened the door into the room Grandma had prepared for me. It was sparse and simple but it would be my personal refuge of sorts, a place to read and to dream. A narrow bed, covered with a purple and pink quilt, an old oak dresser with a mirror and, thankfully, a window looking out into the back forest. I began placing things in the dresser, books and journals in the top drawer with socks and underwear, sweaters and jeans in the next. There was a hook on the back of the door where I hung my flannel nightie. And then I put the photo I had of Mom and Dad, the one where they stood by an old automobile, on my dresser. Glancing in the mirror I was dismayed to see the weight I'd gained at Aunt Lottie's and my hair, once blonde, had dulled to a mousy brown. I wished I could have been a beauty like Grandma was in her time. I would have preferred those deep brown eyes, the ones she and my dad shared, as did Donny and Barb. I tried to recall Mom's eyes, but couldn't. Were they the same glassy sea-green eyes I saw looking back at me?

Joanie

Aunt Lottie and Uncle Jim left the following day after church and I returned to settle into my new life in the old wooden house with so many empty rooms.

"Well, Joan," Grandma said as we finished lunch that day and Grandpa went to his room for a nap. "We haven't had a young girl such as yourself around for some time now. I do hope it won't be too lonely for you living way out here, so far from town and all." She paused, "And it's such a dreadful long walk for you to get to school.

I tried to reassure her. "Well, I want to help you and Grandpa. And besides, Grandma, I have lots of books and I love to read. That is, when the chores are done."

2

That night, taking a candle and mounting the creaky stairs to my room, I felt so vulnerable and alone. Uncle Jim and Aunt Lottie were not in the room down the hall and Grandma and Grandpa seemed so far away in their bedroom downstairs. Reading by candlelight was a challenge so I finally blew out the candle and fell victim to the sounds of the house. My bedroom window rattled in a breeze that whispered through cracks in the glass. I was sure I heard the stairs creaking and light footsteps pacing in the hallways. I barely slept that night and began to dread the nights and the places my imagination took me.

Fitting into a new school presented another challenge. It wasn't the long walk along two concessions and into the village that I disliked. Nor was it the schoolwork itself, which I handled just fine. It was that, in spite of so wanting to fit in and make friends, I found myself shunned.

One morning soon after the semester began we woke to a steady drizzle that looked like it would not let up all day.

"Here, Joan," Grandma insisted. "Wear this old trench coat over your jacket so you don't get wet. Now I know it isn't pretty but I'm sure you'll be grateful for it."

I reluctantly put it on, along with a pair of galoshes that were too big for me. Bowing my head into the drizzle I made my way towards the school. As I approached the village I noticed three of my classmates peering at me from across the road. I noticed one of them point at me saying something that prompted the other two to laugh. Looking down at my shabby oversized clothes I realized that I was the object of their ridicule. I did my best to ignore them and to seek other comrades. But it was a cliquey school. They had all grown up together and were already in their peer groups ranging from most popular to least. I was the new girl, the one that lived out in the country with the old folks. The orphan, some called me. I just couldn't fit in and my days at school were as lonely as the quiet life I endured on the farm.

Joanie

Now that Grandpa was getting older he bought firewood from the man down the road who delivered it, stacking it in neat rows in the woodshed. However Grandpa continued his daily outings back the lane to get kindling wood for the two stoves, the airtight in the parlour and the cook stove in the kitchen. These walks became more and more difficult for him as he became crippled up with arthritis.

One day Grandma suggested that I take on this task. "Joan, you have already been such a big help around here with the cleaning up and all. And I know Grandpa appreciates you looking after those chickens too as it is getting more and more difficult for him to get up and down those stairs." She paused. "But I wonder if you could start gathering the kindling wood for him as well? Now I know the days are getting shorter and soon it will be near dark by the time you get home from school so you won't be able to get some every day like he does. You may have to spend a Saturday afternoon getting enough for the week." She looked at me. "What do you say dear?"

I told her I would be happy to help, looking forward to an outdoor chore. I also wanted to keep busy so my despondency wouldn't run away on me. "Now I should tell you," she added. "There is a tall Indian man who Grandpa sometimes runs into back there. Some say he is not quite right in the head, if you know what I mean."

She paused, wrinkling her brow. "So, I'm telling you, if you see that Indian back there you just come right home. You hear me?"

I assured her I would. But I was actually more intrigued than frightened with the idea of running into an Indian. I was more afraid of ghosts and demons that lived inside of the house, particularly at night when the candle was out. I wasn't afraid of the bush or what I might find there. That's just how I was.

The following Saturday was a bright September day and I looked forward to my afternoon of wood gathering. After a lunch of Grandma's delicious ham and split pea soup I put on a light jacket and prepared for the outing. "Take these as well," Grandpa said, handing me a pair of old leather work gloves. "It will help with breaking the dry branches from the tree."

There was a sharpness in the air, an intoxicating aura of autumn. The maple trees were beginning to turn shades of orange and red and the sweet smell of wood smoke from the fire in the house was delightful. Unfastening the gate I pulled the wagon back the lane, leaving the maple trees and entered a pine forest. Grandpa had told me that the brittle branches from pine trees provide excellent kindling. I began to break some of the driest branches from the trees and load them onto the wagon but then I felt drawn to walk farther back the lane. So leaving the wagon I ventured

Joanie

farther than I had ever been, to where the lane itself was less and less visible and the trees were denser. The stillness was suddenly interrupted by the sound of a grouse that I unknowingly flushed. My heart jumped and my eyes followed him as he found a place high in the pine to roost. Continuing on I found a narrow path that led towards the sound of water. This must be the creek that Grandpa had talked about! I had never been to it but Grandpa said that years ago, before they had a well, he walked way back here to get water. He said the creek didn't freeze in the winter so they could access fresh water year round.

The path was slightly overgrown but the sound of the water lured me on and I easily found the creek. A clear rush of icy water sweeping over patterns of grey and pink rock. The sound of the current mesmerized me and I decided to sit a while and meditate. And then I saw the Indian.

He was walking along the creek and towards me. A towering, dark skinned man, eyes like coal, weathered leathery skin and a wide defined mouth. My heart skipped a beat and I slowly stood up, remembering my promise to Grandma. He looked at me earnestly, not seeming at all surprised by my being there, and said, "Gaakaabishinh. Have you seen Gaakaabishinh?" I slowly shook my head and backed away. "Please," he said, looking at me urgently and reaching his arms out towards me. "Do you know where he is? Have you seen him?"

"N-no," I stammered. "I have not seen him sir." And I turned and quickly walked away.

Grandma was sitting at the kitchen table having a cup of tea when I returned. Pouring myself a cup and standing by the cook stove to warm myself, I told her about my encounter with the Indian man.

"He was looking for somebody Grandma," I said. "He looked so sad and asked if I had seen this person… Gaaabissh…Gaabidish….I can't remember the name. It was a real different name."

"Oh dear," Grandma frowned and wrinkled her brow. "I really don't know if I want you going back into that bush alone. I just don't trust that man."

"But Grandma, he seemed really harmless to me," I encouraged her. "I didn't feel at all threatened by him. He just looked kind of sad. And besides," I added. "I want to help with the wood and I like going back there. It is really pretty."

I was curious about this man and about whom he was looking for and I couldn't stop thinking about him and our brief encounter. I hoped I would see him again. So, the following Saturday I once again left the wagon where I was gathering wood and ventured along the lane and to the path that led to the creek. After some time I heard the rustle of branches and saw the same man walking slowly towards me. This time he greeted me as though he knew me. "Gaakaabinsh," he said. His eyebrows furrowed, "I'm looking for Gaakaabinshih. Have you seen him?"

"No, sir," I said softly. And then I bravely asked, "Who is Gaakaabinshih?"

The man looked at me perplexed, as though surprised that I did not know who he was looking for. And then his eyes welled up and a tear fell down his cheek. With a husky voice he shook his head and said, "They took him away. They took him away somewhere and I can't find where they took him." I took his hand gently, and looked into his troubled eyes. I didn't understand why he was there or who he was looking for but I knew, without a doubt, that I could trust him.

I found Grandpa reading in the parlour when I returned that day and went straight away to talk with him. "Grandpa," I asked. "Do you know who that Indian man is that I have seen back in the bush?"

"Well," he put his book down. "I know he lives in a log cabin on the concession north of here. And I know Grandma worries about him. But I have seen him back there several times and I think he is quite harmless." He paused as though not knowing how far to go with this but then went on. "There was an incident some years ago that I heard about. Not sure exactly what happened but when they came to get his boy to go to that school for Indians up north he refused to let him go. I heard that he just lost it and began striking the officer, insisting they not take his son away. "Well," Grandpa paused. "In some ways you can't blame him, only son and all. Story is someone had to hit him over the head with a garden hoe to stop him." After a moment he said, "So sad. I guess that is why he seems not quite right in the head."

I thought for a moment. "Did his son have a real different name?" I asked. "Something like, 'Gakibish'?

"Well," Grandpa looked thoughtful. "Not that I recollect. I think his boy's name was Josef. I sometimes saw him fishing in the creek back there."

There was a teacher at school that I became fond of. I felt as though he looked out for me knowing I was a misfit of sorts. He occasionally asked if I would stay after school to help him wipe the blackboards and tidy the classroom. I didn't mind at all because we frequently talked about literature and sometimes he would lend me novels that he thought would interest me. One day I caught him off guard during one of our conversations and I asked him why Indians went to a different school.

"Mr. Keating, I heard there is a school up north for Indians."

"Yes," his blue eyes widened and he looked at me thoughtfully.

"But I don't understand why they go to a different school? Why don't they just go to our school?" I asked.

Joanie

"Well, Joan," he hesitated. "This has become a complicated matter and I hope I can answer your question correctly." He continued stacking some papers on his desk. "You know it is government policy for all children in Canada to attend school, don't you?"

I nodded.

"And you, know of course, the value of education?"

"Yes."

"Well," he went on. "The government decided that it would benefit Indian children to learn how to read and write like every other child in Canada. This was some time ago. And so they built these residential schools, as they are called."

This wasn't answering my question but I wanted to be respectful to Mr. Keating.

"But, sir." I was confused. "Why couldn't they go to our schools and learn to read and write?"

"Well, this is the part that I am not totally sure about but I think that the belief at the time was that they would learn English better if they were not living at home with their families and speaking their native tongues."

I thought of what Grandpa had told me about the Indian man and about them coming to take his son away to school. And I wondered if his son could have felt like me when he found himself alone in a strange place without his parents. Not everyone had it all like Lily Barns, the most popular girl in the class. She lived in the pretty white house across the road from the school. Her mother and father owned the hotel in town. She had lots of friends and was already going out on dates. I wondered about the fairness of things. I thanked Mr. Keating and set off on my long walk home.

3

The following two Saturdays found me sitting down by the creek, wrapped snugly in Grandma's old wool jacket and waiting to see if the Indian man would come. There was a bite in the air; frost, the coming of winter. It was already mid October and most of the leaves had fallen from the maples creating a tapestry of colour on the ground. I swished playfully through the leaves as I made my way towards the pine forest and the creek, expectantly. However, those Saturdays found me alone with my thoughts and disappointed. No welcome intruders to break the silence of the afternoons and to distract me from my aloneness. I fell into a melancholy of sorts going about my chores ritually and escaping into stories of romance and adventure when I had the time. It wasn't until one Saturday in November I was drawn there once more.

We awoke to the first snowfall that morning. The cosmos, once so brilliant, were bending with the cold and the redpolls were scrambling in their search for any accessible seedlings. But it was a stunning morning. The sky was a brilliant blue and sunshine illuminated the carpet of white. The air was sharp and I felt a new energy with the changing of the seasons.

The pine forest was especially pretty that morning, snow hanging delicately on branches. I left my wagon, full with kindling for another week, and headed towards the creek. There was a sweet smell of wood smoke in the air and I was surprised to see someone sitting around a campfire on the creek bed. Deafened by the sound of the current they did not hear me approach. However I stumbled over a few rocks and was surprised that it was not the Indian man who turned and looked at me but someone much younger. My heart stood still as I saw a dark-skinned boy, not much older than me, return my gaze.

I suddenly felt foolish and sorry for intruding. "I'm sorry," I said, looking down at my feet. "I didn't mean to surprise you."

He didn't say anything and I noticed he had been eating a fish that he had cooked over the fire. He slowly tore a piece from the carcass and offered it to me.

"Thank you." I said enjoying the smoky tasting fish. "Its good. What kind is it?"

"I think you call it 'rainbow trout'. But it is 'Namegos', in my language."

"Nameeeegos," I said it all wrong and he laughed, a quick, gentle laugh. His large dark eyes confronted me. "Sit," he said. It was direct yet welcoming. I curled up by the fire suddenly embarrassed by the old wool coat.

We didn't talk. We simply sat by the fire sharing the fish. The silence felt a bit awkward at first but then I kind of got used to it. After we finished the fish he put a tea bag in a pot of fresh creek water and placed it on the fire. "I'll make tea," he said.

I wanted to ask him who he was. Was he the son of the man I had been seeing there? If so, why he was not at one of those Indian schools? But there was just this silence and words seemed foreign and intrusive to sound of the creek and the fire.

He poured the tea into a blue enamel mug and we passed it back and forth sharing it. And then I stood to leave, knowing that Grandma would be beginning to worry about me. "Thank you for the fish and for the tea," I said putting my hand out to him. He took my hand gently and said, "I'm Josef." I smiled and replied, "Hello Josef. I am Joan."

And then I turned and walked quickly back to get the wagon of wood and along the lane towards the farm. The sun had melted most of the snow on the open fields and a flock of geese were honking in flight above me. The light of day was fading, bewitching in its transformation of day to night. I had a song in my heart.

It seemed like forever until the next Saturday arrived. The week at school was long and tedious and the nights in the blackness of my room were never ending. My imagination wavered between visits from ghosts who occupied the empty rooms down the hall to reliving the scene with Josef by the creek. I tried to meditate on the tick of the clock that was taking me to unseen places. But try as I might, sleep would not wrap his huge safe arms around me and I lay awake for hours.

Finally it was Saturday and I anticipated the afternoon when I would venture back into the woods. Grandma must have sensed something.

"You seem unusually chipper this morning," she said smiling at me as I cleared the breakfast dishes away. "And I must say it is nice to see you smiling rather than moping about the house." And then, "Have you made a new friend at school?"

I looked down at my feet thinking of all of the stuck-up girls and uninteresting boys in my class. "No, Grandma. No, I haven't."

"Oh," she raised an eyebrow. "Well, that's too bad." She sighed. "I know it is a lonely life for you here dear."

"It's ok, Grandma," I assured her. "It is nice to be with you and Grandpa." And I slipped away to my room, which was a much friendlier place in the light of day.

It was as though he knew I would come and I found him sitting in the same place that Saturday afternoon. A skiff of snow was melting around the perimeter of the campfire and a light breeze waved the smoke across the creek. He turned as I approached and smiled. "I brought an extra mug in case you came," he said, invitingly.

This time I had dressed more carefully. I put two wool sweaters on rather than the bulky old coat I normally wore. And I found a bright red scarf that I wound around my neck. I covered my obnoxiously large ears with a pair of earmuffs that I found somewhat flattering. Still I was shivering in the November afternoon and the fire was a welcome refuge.

"Hi Josef," I said shyly, curling up by the fire.

He poured a cup of tea and handed it to me. It tasted different this time. "Spruce tip tea," he said. It had a tangy fresh taste and I was amazed that you could make tea from the trees. "Wow," I said. "It's good."

We sat in contemplative silence, even though millions of questions about him and his life were running through my head. And then he stood and asked if I would like to walk with him. "Sure," I said, standing as well, now flushed from the warmth of the fire.

He led me along the creek as it curled through the mixed pine and spruce forest, singing and splashing over rocks. It was like an adventure, following this trail into other worlds. The sun peeped through the upper branches and illuminated the water in silvers and greys. I felt lightheaded and spontaneously decided to jump across the creek. But I tripped and fell, cutting my knee on a sharp rock. Blood oozed from the wound and Josef quickly took a handkerchief out of his pocket and wiped away the blood. He told me to wait by the creek and disappeared into the forest. When he returned her put a yellowish sticky substance on the cut. "Spruce pitch," he said. It will clean the wound." And then, "Pitch is an important medicine for my people."

I nodded, in wonder. Wonder of this boy and of the idea of making medicine and tea from trees. I didn't know what to say. I just followed him as we walked quietly through the maze of forest and water. Finally I said I should go back.

"My grandma will worry if I am not home soon," I said apologetically.

I turned to leave and he said, "I will walk you back to your lane." I was grateful for his company feeling slightly uneasy in this unknown place. But I was also aware of his eyes on me as he followed me and my heart skipped a beat.

We reached the wagon, which I had parked beneath the familiar maple. I traced my fingers along the initials in the tree and he looked at me inquisitively. "This was where my mom and dad used to come," I shared with him. He nodded, waiting. "They both died when I was young."

"That must have been hard," he said. Again, no questions, just this warmth in his voice and I suddenly felt like talking. He sat down beneath the old tree and I knelt beside him. I hadn't talked with anyone about all of it before. About having little recollection of my mom and about how I loved my dad so much. And about Mary and the way I missed her after she left. And I told him about my horrible cousin Barbara and about not feeling wanted by her mom or my Aunt Lottie. It all came out, all of those dreadful memories that haunted me day and night, that feeling of not belonging and of being so alone. I found myself crying and he removed a handkerchief from his pocket and handed it to me quietly. It felt so good to just let the tears fall beneath that old maple tree and in the company of this strange boy. But I finally noticed the light of day fading.

"I really must go," I said, slowly rising. He stood as well and took my hand. "Thank you," I whispered looking deeply into his dark eyes. "Maybe I'll see you next week?"

He smiled and nodded.

Pulling the wagon home I felt somehow lighter inside but also very tired. Grandma was looking out the kitchen window for me. "Where in land's sake have you been, child?" she said as I entered the room and warmed myself by the stove. "Grandpa and I have been worried about you. Did you see that Indian back there?"

Grandpa was looking in at us from the hallway. "No," I said. "But I met Josef, his son." I looked at Grandpa and paused. "And, we talked. I'm sorry Grandma. But I just lost track of time."

"Oh Joan," Grandma frowned. "I just don't know if I want you spending time with that boy." She paused. "He's different from us." She looked at Grandpa and then turned back to me. "It would be better if you made friends with someone at school."

A voice inside my head said, "No. No, you can't take this away from me." But instead I flatly said, "Grandma, I have tried to make friends at school. I honestly have." I bowed my head and felt my eyes well with tears. "But I just don't fit in there. No one likes me."

"Now, now dear," Grandma put her arms around me and drew me towards her. "It can't be that bad. It will just take some time. I'm sure you will make friends eventually." Then, in an attempt to change the subject, she smiled and said, "Now why not set the table for supper? I have some beef stew and fresh bread to warm you up."

4

The days dragged on that week as I methodically walked the mile and a half to school doing my best to ignore any rude stares from my classmates. On two occasions I remained after school to help Mr. Keating and to discuss our latest literature assignment. And then I returned home to an evening of chores and homework. It was uneventful and tiring but the nights were much worse as I tossed and turned all night in and out of sleep going over our talk under the old maple tree. Sometimes I'd wake in terror from the same recurring nightmare. There was this table all set for dinner in an old house not unlike this one. But no one was there. And there was some unexplainable terror around this abandonment. It seemed like forever until the welcome grey light of dawn peeked through my bedroom window and I found myself another day closer to Saturday.

When I found Josef by the creek that Saturday he was distraught. He was pacing back and forth by the campfire, like a caged wild animal. He looked at me blackly as I walked towards him, no smile this week, no welcoming mug of tea. I stood there quietly, not understanding why this sudden change.

"They sent a letter," he said, a sharp edge in his voice. "They 'demanded' that I return to the school."

I didn't know what to say. But I somehow felt his pain.

"But I won't go," he said, angrily tossing a branch in the fire. "I won't go back there."

"Well, they can't make you, can they?" I quietly asked, looking down at the fire.

"They say they can," he breathed. "They said if I don't return on my own immediately, they will send someone from the school to bring me back."

He took some bannock and dried fish out of an old canvas backpack and offered me some. The bannock tasted just like the fried biscuits Grandma made in the old cast iron pan. I wasn't very hungry but took some and slowly began chewing the dried fish.

"My mom and dad need me," he went on. "I help them a lot with the wood and all and I fish and hunt for them."

"I think I met your dad," I looked up at him. "Down here by the creek."

He looked back at me, inquisitively.

"I think he was looking for you," I added.

Bitterly he told me what I already knew, about the officer that hit his father over the head when he came to take Josef away. And about the damage it caused to his brain. "It's not fair," he blurted out. "It's just not fair. They hurt him. They made him sick. And now they don't understand. I'm 14 years old now and I need to be there to help him, to help him and my ma."

After a few quiet moments I ventured, "He called you a different name, when I saw him here," I looked at him. "Gabridesh, gabridesh, or something."

Finally, he smiled. That welcome wide smile that lit up his dark face. "'Gaakaabinsh'," he said. "It means 'screech owl'. My mom called me that because the night I was born there was a screech owl outside the window. She said it was flying back and forth attracted to the light from the candle."

We sat quietly for quite some time and his anger dissipated into a melancholy of sorts. He poked away at the fire staring into the bright flames that reflected off his dark eyes. He was not finished talking.

"It's not just that," he said.

I waited, feeling he wanted to say something.

"Its just that I hate it there. I can't sleep at night." And then, "It's a terrible place and terrible things happen there."

"Like what?" I asked.

He paused and looked at me. "I can't talk about it," he said looking down at the fire again. "Only, I have these nightmares," his voice trailed off.

"Me too," I said in an attempt to show some understanding. "I have this dream almost every night and

I wake up so scared." I paused and looked over at him. "I – I don't sleep a lot anyway. I hate the nights."

He sighed and smiled at me. "Well, Joan. Maybe you and I are not so different after all," he said standing and reaching for my hand.

He walked me back to the wagon and lightly touched my elbow before turning to go. Shivering I pulled the wagon full of wood through the skiff of snow as the light of day faded. And thankfully there were no anxious questions to greet me at home. Grandma was standing by the wood cook stove frying biscuits. She poured me a cup of hot tea.

"Here child" she said. "Warm up with some tea."

I smiled at her, grateful there was not to be an interrogation. And feeling honoured somehow that Josef had confided in me. I wanted to keep this secret of him deep inside, to treasure it and to respect it. I sipped on the tea as I watched Grandma turn each biscuit carefully in the hot oil.

5

That week, the first week of December, there was a dreadful snowstorm. The wind howled all night as the snow blew in drifts around the barn and house. I barely slept at all listening to the fury it all and wondering what the world would look like in the morning. But after I finally did get some sleep I woke to a brilliant blue sky and the calm that follows a winter storm. Looking outside my bedroom window I saw the snow piled high against the fence and wondered how I would manage with the wood on Saturday.

"What a night," Grandma said as I came down the stairs. "I haven't seen so much snow fall like that for a long time."

I shivered and went over to the stove to warm up. A pot of porridge was in the warming oven and I helped myself to a large bowl feeling hungry after a night of tossing and turning.

Grandpa was out shovelling the walk way and I realized that it might be a more challenging walk to school that day. I quickly finished my porridge and dressed in a warm wool sweater and jeans before putting on the bulky old wool coat and oversized boots.

"Poor child," Grandma muttered as I merged out into the fresh, deep snow. But I found the walk to school to be not so difficult after all. The roads had been ploughed and I found myself entranced as I walked under the brilliant blue sky, sunlight illuminating the brightness of the fresh snow.

Saturday came and we were just finishing lunch when Grandpa said, "Well, Barbara, maybe I should try to split some of those big logs into kindling wood today. It will be too hard for Joan to get back in the woods with all that snow."

I had expected something like this and presented Grandpa with an option. "Grandpa, what about that old toboggan in the barn? Maybe I could put a few boxes on that and pull it back in the snow?"

"Still, Joan," he said, scratching the stubble of grey beard on his chin, "It will be hard for you to get through the snow yourself. It's deep out there especially where it has drifted by the fence."

"But I want to Grandpa." I hesitated. "And, if it is too difficult then perhaps I could try splitting some wood for you. Its hard for you to do it with your arthritis."

So it was agreed that I would give it a try and I was soon plunging through near knee-deep snow pulling the old toboggan behind me. The toboggan made a decent trail so I was encouraged that it would be an easier walk home. The dry branches were especially brittle that day with the plunging temperatures and I had soon filled the two boxes. Then, expectantly, I made my way to the creek.

But there was no one there. I waited for almost an hour shivering as I buried my gloved hands deep into my pockets and stomped my feet to keep them from freezing. It was a dreadful hour spent waiting and I finally accepted that he wouldn't come. Dismayed, I returned home wondering if he had been forced to return to the school.

The following day, another bright sunny day, I told Grandma that I felt like going for a walk.

"Heavens, child," she said. "Don't you do enough walking all week going to and from school? Besides, where would you go on such a day?"

"I'm not sure Grandma. But it is a beautiful day and the roads should be clear enough to walk on."

I didn't tell her that I actually did have a plan in mind. I anticipated looking for the little log cabin that Grandpa had talked about. I wanted to see for myself if Josef had in fact returned to the school.

I hadn't walked that way before but found the concession north of ours in no time. A large dairy farm sprawled across the junction of the two roads and, as I turned on to the concession, several cows lifted their heads watching me inquisitively. Making my way along the road I noticed the familiar mixed forest I knew from my wood gathering expeditions. Then the creek, sparkling away as it plummeted under the bridge. And then I saw, set in a grove of spruce trees not far from the creek, a small log cabin, smoke curling as it rose from the chimney and a skidoo parked outside.

My stomach was turning in knots and I wondered at my tenacity in coming. I mean, who was I to intrude on

Joanie

their space? Besides, I wasn't even sure this was the right place. I thought about turning back but then saw Josef's father come outside to get an armful of firewood. Lifting his head he noticed me watching him from the road so I waved and approached him. He stood quietly and smiled at me. "Is Josef here?" I asked timidly.

He lifted his eyebrows, looking confused. Then, without speaking, he motioned me inside. Seated at a table in the corner of the cabin was an attractive woman sewing a pair of moccasins. Her long dark hair was slung over one shoulder and she looked up at me, eyes as black as Josef's, and smiled.

"Have some tea," she said, pointing towards a teapot on the table. "Mugs are in the cupboard." She nodded towards a hutch that was against the far wall.

I found a mug and poured some tea. "I'm sorry to bother you," I said, sitting down at the table across from her. "I was wondering if Josef was here?"

Her eyes darkened and she looked down at her sewing. "No," she said, sighing. "I'm afraid he had to return to the school."

"Gaakaabinsh, Gaakaabinsh went away," Josef's father muttered from the couch across the room. "They came and took him away." And then, as if forgetting what he just said, "Do you know where he is?"

"No, sir," I said sadly, looking at him and remembering how much Josef wanted to remain home to help him. "I have not seen him since last week."

The dark haired woman looked up at me and smiled. "You must be Joan."

I was surprised, in a way that he had told her about me. But I was also happy that he had and I nodded.

"I used to see him down by the creek when I was gathering firewood. Sometimes we went for a walk together or had tea by the fire." I paused. "He told me about the school and about how he didn't want to go back. He wanted to stay and help you and his dad."

"I am Gabriella," Josef's mom said, standing. She looked down at me. "Have some soup with us."

She motioned for Josef's dad to come to the table. "This is my husband Johnny." She took his hand and looked at him. "Joan," she said, pointing to me.

"Joan." His warm eyes gazed at me and flashed, perhaps with some recollection of seeing me before. "Joan."

I glanced around the cabin and was taken with the pure simplicity of it. A large barrel stove divided the kitchen area from a sitting room of sorts. A fire crackled in the stove and the sun shone through two tall narrow windows illuminating the gold of the logs. Bright striped blankets decorated two of the walls and family photos were organized on another wall. The wide plank pine floor had been swept clean and a bright red curtain closed off what I presumed to be a bedroom.

Gabriella put some soup in front of me and laughed, "Have you ever had rabbit soup before?" She winked at her husband. "Johnny sets snares for them and he checks his little trap line every day." She sighed. "We are actually getting tired of eating rabbit. But I make sure to thank the Creator every day for what he provides for us. Still, if Josef were here we would have a better chance of eating fresh deer meat."

The soup had a wild, tangy flavour and the meat was very tender. Gabriella said she was happy to have some female company and talked freely about her sewing projects and different recipes she had for wild meat. Then, being curious about Josef I asked if she had ever been to the school to see him. Her face darkened and she whispered, "Only once."

We sat quietly for a few moments and she went on to say, "Families are not allowed to visit the school. They say that they want the children to focus their attention totally on their schoolwork and not be distracted by family visits." She paused. "But, only once we went there. We – we had to pick up our daughter."

"Oh," my eyes widened. "Josef never mentioned that he had a sister."

Gabriella's face darkened, "She died," she whispered, looking down at her empty bowl. "She became sick at the school, not long after she was taken there. She was six years old and Josef was seven." She paused. "They said it was diphtheria. They called for us to come and take her home."

I didn't know what to say. I couldn't imagine her pain. I just looked into her deep, dark eyes and reached my hand out to hers. A few tears welled in her eyes and Johnny, looking distraught at her sudden show of emotion came to her side and put his large gentle arms around her. I felt as though there was a lot of love and sadness in this little house.

We sat in silence for a while and then, feeling I should head back, I rose and took Johnny's hand. "It was nice to see you again sir," I said. And then I went to Gabriella and embraced her warmly, "Thank you so much for the lunch and for the visit."

She held me for a few moments and then said, "Wait. I have something for you."

She disappeared into the room behind the curtain and returned with something I had not seen before. "Josef was making this for you," she said handing me an attractive beaded object. "It's called a dream-catcher." She went on to say, "Our people are Ojibwa. We crafted these. Hang it somewhere by your bedside and it will catch your bad dreams and only let good dreams reach you."

I smiled, remembering that I had told Josef about my nightmares. How thoughtful of him.

"I think he was hoping to give it to you at Christmas this year." She paused and looked sad, "But I don't think he will be able to come home for Christmas." Bitterly, she added, "School policy."

I put on my old wool coat and smiled at her. "Come back Joan," she said, encouragingly.

"I would like that," I said, slipping the dream catcher under my coat to keep it warm and safe.

And I did come back. I returned the following two Sundays and enjoyed my visits with Gabriella and Johnny. Gabriella told me a lot about her people, about some of their traditional foods and medicines and about summer gatherings they called pow-wows that were alive with song and dance. She proudly told me that her people were originally from the shores of Lake Superior but were moved by the Canadian government to the Coldwater area as part of an experiment, to see if they would adjust to farming.

"The Coldwater Project, they called it," she snickered. "Imagine. Our people were hunters and gatherers. The bush was our livelihood. Fish, moose, deer, berries and medicines were all a huge part of our life. We did not grow things. We did not stand still." She was silent for a few moments. "So you see, their so called 'experiment' failed. They thought they could appease us by giving us all a little piece of land to farm. But owning land is foreign to us. It is like owning the air or the water — or sunlight. These things are all gifts from the Creator. We believe these things are meant for us to share, not to own."

I watched her as she spoke with such passion of these things. I was at an impressionable age and I found myself fascinated by her - so different from anyone I had met before. Her earthly values and simple lifestyle challenged many of the things I had grown up with. Things like getting a job, making money, owning land. I pondered these things day and night as I explored just who I was and who I was becoming. And I wondered at how I felt such an outcast by peers at school yet so warmly accepted by these new friends, whose world was so different from mine.

6

It was a gentle snow that fell that Christmas morning. I looked out my bedroom window to see a dance of snowflakes floating softly to the ground. I touched the dream-catcher that hung by the window feeling some comfort in this simple gift. It had been a huge disappointment to learn that Aunt Alice wouldn't be bringing Barb up for the holidays. There had been some talk of the whole family coming and I had so hoped to see the quiet, empty house suddenly infused with life. However they decided the trip would be too costly.

Coming down the stairs I could hear Grandma in the parlour fussing with a radio Grandpa had recently bought her for an early Christmas present. "There must be some Christmas music on this," she was muttering to herself. Soon she located a station and 'Hark the Herald Angels' chorused throughout the house.

"Merry Christmas, Grandma," I wound my arms around her and hugged her. She felt warm in her long flannel nightgown.

"And to you, dear," she said smiling and returning my squeeze. Even though Grandma was 70 years old those dark brown eyes still twinkled with a childish excitement over Christmas.

"I've got some hot cross buns warming in the oven and Grandpa is just getting dressed. Let's have a bite and then we can open our gifts."

I went into the pantry and poured a glass of orange juice. A small turkey was thawing on the sideboard along with a fresh berry pie Grandma had been saving for Christmas. I knew she would do all she could to make this day special, knowing how disappointed I was about Barb not coming. And I was grateful.

After breakfast we went into the parlour where the new radio continued to blast an assortment of carols. A small pine tree stood beside the old pump organ. I had insisted that I bring one back on the sled for our Christmas, "Just like you did with Dad when he was little," I said to Grandpa. We'd decorated it with strings of cranberries and popcorn and a few candles that, when lit, lent an element of magic to the room.

Under the tree were some wrapped gifts and I anticipated giving them both the scarves I had crocheted for them. Grandma first opened hers, a pretty lilac colour, and wound it around her neck. "It is just lovely, Joanie," she said. "Now I know what you have been doing all those hours up in your room."

"Thank you Joan," Grandpa said warmly as he unwrapped his charcoal grey one. "Homemade gifts are always the most special." He winked at me.

Grandma handed me a large box wrapped carefully in bright red paper. "This is for you dear. I hope you like it."

Opening the box I gasped in surprise. Folded neatly inside was a lovely red, wool coat. It was the prettiest coat I had ever seen. I immediately stood up and put it on over my pyjamas, fastening the large black buttons and winding the belt around me. I knew this would have cost them more than they could afford. "I love it," I exclaimed, hugging them both tightly. I knew I would never forget this Christmas.

The following day I felt drawn to visit Gabriella and Johnny. I had been apprehensive about telling Grandma about this new friendship knowing she would discourage it on the basis that they were 'different' than us. So I simply told her that I enjoyed my afternoon walks and not to worry about me if I was gone most of the afternoon.

"You are wearing your new coat on the walk?" Grandma asked as I buttoned up my treasured gift.

I laughed, "Yes I just can't wait to try it out," I said.

I put on a navy scarf, which complimented the bright red wool and, glancing in the hall mirror I was pleased to see how the colour accentuated my high cheekbones. I had lost some weight with all of my wood gathering and walking and grown my hair longer so it covered my ears and nicely framed my face. I was growing taller and into myself and felt some relief in leaving the plump forlorn girl behind.

Johnny was just coming in from his daily walk on the trap line when I arrived. His face lit up when he saw me and he proudly showed me the rabbit he had snared.

"Joan," he said beaming and obviously pleased that he remembered my name.

I took his hand and said, "I hope you had a nice Christmas Johnny."

We went inside and the cabin was warm and cozy. Gabriella immediately admired my new coat.

"You look lovely," she said coming over to give me a hug. "And I'm so happy you came."

I told her about our Christmas and about how Grandma tried so hard to make it special. "It was the nicest Christmas I've had since my dad died," I said, suddenly feeling guilty that I wasn't being truthful with Grandma about my afternoon walks.

"I'm happy for you child," Gabriella said as she poured three cups of tea. She sighed, "I must say it was a lonely day for Johnny and I. We sure missed Josef."

I nodded.

Then she tossed her head and laughed. "But we did have a delicious dinner didn't we Johnny?" He looked at her inquisitively. "Johnny shot a grouse and we boiled it on the stove all Christmas Day so it was nice and tender."

"There was a time we would go to church on Christmas," she went on to say. "Before Johnny was hurt, that is. We used to have an old pick-up back then and would drive into Coldwater for the Christmas Eve service." She paused, reflecting. "That was when Johnny could drive and we were able to get out more."

Johnny was fussing with the zipper on his sweater, which was stuck. "Here, let me help you." Gabriella went to him and managed to set it right.

Joanie

"I liked going to the service," she said. "Only I did find it strange, the idea of worshipping in a building and only once a week. I mean, I pray every day, actually several times a day. Prayer is simply a part of our life. Just like the air we breathe."

She sipped on her tea and looked at me thoughtfully. "I remember asking my Grandpa about God when I was a child. One day as we were walking through the woods I looked up at him and asked, 'Grandpa, who is God?'" My Grandfather paused and thought for a moment and then, tightening his grip on my hand, he looked down at me and said the simplest thing. 'Granddaughter, He is your very breath.'"

"So that stuck with me. Grandpa's wisdom. And I am thankful for it. And for all that he taught me."

I reflected on it. "He is your very breath." I liked it. I liked the way her Grandfather thought about God and I liked the way Gabriella brought these stories alive before my eyes.

As I prepared to leave that day Gabriella went into the back room and brought back a letter. "Its for you," she said smiling. "From Josef."

My heart leapt and I placed it deep in the pocket of my new coat. "Thank you," I said hugging her and Johnny in turn, suddenly eager to go home and to the privacy of my room.

I walked with a north wind at my back all the way home but I was snug in my new coat, with my hands buried deep in the pockets, one clasping the letter.

Grandma was in the kitchen preparing dinner. "Have a fresh biscuit," she said as I entered the warmth of the kitchen.

"Thanks but I think I will save my appetite for dinner Grandma," I said taking off my gloves and warming my hands over the stove. "If you don't need any help maybe I'll go and lie down for a bit."

"Go ahead, Joan. Dinner is in the oven and will be ready in about an hour."

Escaping to my room I sat on my bed and read.

Joan

> When they came to take me back to the school that day I thought of you. I wished I could have somehow let you know I wouldn't be at the creek. But I had no way of reaching you. It was awful leaving. Mom cried and Dad just stood by shaking his head, confused, while one of them stood next to him to make sure he didn't do anything stupid.
>
> I hate it here. I hate it so much. I miss Mom and Dad. I miss speaking

our language and I miss the food we eat at home; the wild meat and fish and the berries. Here we eat a watery porridge every morning for breakfast and usually a bland soup for lunch and dinner that tastes awful. But the nights are the worst. Terrible things happen during the nights. Horrible things.

Mom wrote and told me that you have been visiting them. I am so glad you go and see them. They are lonely and look forward to your visits. Did you like the dream-catcher? Are you still having those nightmares?

I hope you are okay and had a nice Christmas. I can't wait for summer to come when I can go home again. And hopefully we can go for more walks together and go fishing and exploring.

I would love to hear from you if you feel like writing to me at the address on this envelope. Until then,

Josef (Gaabaakinsh)

I put the letter under my pillow rather than in the top drawer where I kept all of my letters from Barb and Donny and Mary. I knew I would read it again and again.

I looked up at the dream catcher. I still had the nightmare occasionally but when I woke from it I felt some comfort in knowing the dream catcher was hanging there.

Later that night, by candlelight, I scratched,

> Gaabaahinsh (Josef),
>
> I think your mom is amazing. I love hearing her stories and I feel I learn so much from her. I know she misses you very much. And your dad does too. I think you look a lot like him. He is such a sweet and gentle man and I have been happy to get to know them (and you).
>
> We had a quiet Christmas but it was nice to be with Grandma and Grandpa. I was hoping Barb would come up but they couldn't afford the trip. We didn't have a wild grouse like your parents did but had a delicious turkey with all the trimmings.
>
> I hung the dream-catcher you made above my bed and it comforts me during the nights. Thank you so much. It is very special.
>
> Yes, I waited at the creek that day for some time. Of course I was disappointed but it was much worse for you — having

to go back there. I just don't understand it. I don't understand why you can't go to the same school I do or why you couldn't at least come home to your parents for Christmas.

But I guess there are a lot of things that are beyond our understanding and we can only live one day at a time and hope for the best. I look forward to seeing you when you are able to come home again. Until then I will keep writing to you and I will look forward to your letters if you choose to write again.

Yours truly,
Joan.

A few weeks later Gabriella handed me another letter from Josef. This time I didn't wait until I got home. It was a bright day, and in spite of being late January there was some warmth from the sun. I found a quiet place by the creek to open the letter

Joan,

I feel there is no one I can talk to here. I am getting to know some of the other students but they are also struggling with being here. So I hope you don't mind if I talk to you. Maybe it will help to write some of this down. I don't know. I usually keep things to myself. But I feel this rage growing inside of me and I don't know what to do with it. Maybe writing to you will help.

When I first came here I was six years old. My little sister, Aandeg, was five. She cried for mom all the way here on the bus. I remember holding her hand tightly as we entered the school. I thought we would at least be able to stay together. But as soon as we got here a nun came to take her to the girls' side of the school. She screamed when they took her away from me and the nun became really cross and told her to be quiet. I didn't see her much after that. Boys and girls were separated.

First they shaved our heads in case we had lice. They didn't even check first to see if we did. Then they took our clothes away and told us to have a shower and put on school uniforms. With our shaved heads and identical uniforms we all looked much the same. Next we were lined up and all given English names. We were instructed to not speak our native languages and were warned that, if we did, we would be strapped. I knew some English words when I arrived because Mom and Dad had also been forced to learn English at residential schools. But I was not comfortable with the language. We rarely used it at home unless we had an English-speaking visitor.

I remember feeling so lonely and scared. Everything was strange and foreign. At night I would lie in bed and dream of home and suddenly realize my face was wet with tears. I hope you don't mind me writing all of this to you but I think of you sometimes and of what you told me. About when your mom and dad died and you had to live with your aunt and the cousin who was mean to you. I can only imagine how lonely you must have felt for your parents and for the life you once had. At least my parents are still alive. Maybe I want to tell you these things because I think you might somehow understand. Anyway, thanks for listening and I will write more later. I hope I hear from you soon.

Josef.

I was shivering with the cold when I finished reading the letter. I folded it quickly and rose to leave, plunging my hands deep in my pockets. And then I found myself crying —crying for the terrible things that happened to Josef and his sister and crying for my mom and dad and for the way I missed them.

Later that day I escaped to my room to write back to him. It seemed like some kind of therapy, being able to expose these wounds I had buried for so long. To finally express myself to another person and especially to someone who seemed to have some empathy and understanding for what I had been through.

> Josef,
>
> I can't imagine what it would be like to live in such a place — so far away from your family and your home. I am really sorry those things had to happen to you. But I am happy that you felt comfortable enough to tell me about it. You're right when you say that I can somehow understand how you must feel. The difference is that you have had a 'rage growing inside of you' and I would say for years I have not felt much at all. It is more like a dream, thinking of my mom's casket in the living room of

our house. And of my dad kneeling there, beside her, sobbing. I remember feeling numb and only began feeling things again when Mary brought some brightness into our lives. But it didn't last. When Dad died the numbness returned. I remember hardly crying at all. And it wasn't that I didn't love him. Oh – I loved him so much. He was so large and full of life. But when he left us it was like a switch turned off in me. I was moved around to different relatives and I didn't feel wanted by anyone. I tried not to let it all matter.

When I read your letter I cried. Like I said, I can't remember crying much before. But it felt good to cry. I think I need to somehow let it all out — all of those things buried deep inside of me. Maybe the 'numbness' is my way of coping. So, thank you Josef for sharing your story with me. And thank you for listening to mine.

> Your friend,
> Joan

7

Winter gave way to the soft hues of spring. The snow began to melt and migrating birds returned from their winter ranges. Robins welcomed each bright morning in song as swallows darted around in pursuit of nest building materials. The longer days and warmth from the sun was rejuvenating and I marvelled at the miracles of nature — the mud nests that suddenly appeared on the eves of the barn and the sprouts of daffodils poking up in the garden that ran alongside the farmhouse. I was especially positive because we were planning a trip to the city.

"Aunt Alice has invited us for Easter," Grandma had told me one day as I came in from school. "And Uncle Roy will be coming up with the family as well."

This would mean I would see Barb and Donny! I hadn't seen either in over two years. I could hardly wait.

And so, on a bright Good Friday morning Grandpa warmed up the old Plymouth that had not been running for some time and we were on our way. I wore my new wool coat, in spite of it being warmer, because it was the nicest thing I had. It was a two-hour drive to the outskirts of the city and I gazed out the window watching farmland merge into suburbs and the high-rises of downtown Toronto. Admittedly there was some excitement in entering the city. However I knew that my heart had been claimed by the sound of fresh creek water and the smell of the forest.

We pulled up outside of the stoic, old brick house on Annette Street. As we opened the door into the foyer I heard a squeal from upstairs and Barb flew down the steep narrow staircase.

"Joanie, Joanie," she cried jumping into my arms. Her face was wet with tears of joy and I embraced her warmly and wondered at my own return to joy.

"Let me look at you," I laughed, holding her away from me. Her face was flushed and her eyes bright and I saw that she was growing into a very pretty young girl, tall and slim with golden curls framing her dark brown eyes and delicate cheekbones.

Aunt Alice gave me a quick hug and told me to take my things up to Barb's room. "I'm afraid you will have to share Barb's bed, Joan. There is really nowhere else."

Barb shared the room with two of my cousins, Joyce and Jean. There was an assortment of jewelry and makeup covering two dressers and clothes strewn all around the room. Still, it was bright and friendly and a startling comparison to my lonely room in the old farmhouse.

Barb closed the door and motioned for me to sit on the bed with her. "Joyce and Jean are out shopping right now so we can have some time to ourselves."

Words flooded out of her mouth. She talked about how much she'd missed me and how she'd never felt completely at home with Aunt Alice. "Its true. She has been good to me," she sighed. "But it's just that I am the youngest and I don't think the other girls like me so well. I mean I don't think Joyce and Jean wanted to share their room with me and the others just kind of ignore me."

Most of this she had already relayed to me in letters. But it seemed like she needed to tell me in person. I listened and reminded her that I had a similar experience with Aunt Pearl and cousin Barbara. "I know it's an awful feeling, not feeling wanted," I said. "But I guess we can only be thankful that we have a place to stay and try to make the best of it."

We heard some commotion downstairs and went down to see Donny standing in the doorway, a wide smile spread across his face. "There you two are," he said opening his arms to us. We all three hugged and I felt safe and loved. Donny, now 15 years old, had grown tall and lean. He looked more like Dad. It was a strange sensation, leaning into him and thinking of my Dad.

And then the house became alive as Grandma and my aunts prepared dinner and the girls came home from shopping. There was an exchange of greetings and a flurry of activity. I hardly recognized most of my cousins but we all chatted about the paths our lives had taken and they

Joanie

spoke of their future aspirations. They were older than Barb and I and their lives seemed bright and alive with purpose and direction.

Later that night, after Barb fell asleep curled up close beside me, I lay awake thinking about it all. Their lives were definitely full and interesting. And this was by no means a lonely house. I wouldn't even think about the possibility of ghosts and spirits haunting these hallways. And yet, the simple and rustic life of the farm somehow appealed to me. I thought of Josef and of Gabriella. Both seemed million of miles away. But in fact, they were a lifetime away. They lived such a different life than these lives I had walked in on in the city. And I wondered which seemed more real? For me I knew it was the farm.

It was a busy and happy weekend filled with board games, card games and meals shared around two tables. Barb and Donny and I crowded around the kitchen table with our cousins, all teenagers now, while the adults conversed around the table in the dining room. In spite of Barb's trepidation I became friends with my cousin Joyce, who was not much older than me. She was a model of warmth and kindness. Before we left we agreed to remain in touch and exchange letters.

On Sunday morning we all went to church and returned to Aunt Alice's for a lunch of leftover turkey and ham. Then we prepared to leave. Saying goodbye, once more, to Barb and Donny was hard.

"Maybe Aunt Alice will let you come to the farm in the summer," I whispered to Barb as I buttoned my coat up by the front door. But Barb was bowing her head crying and between the tears she sobbed, "No, she probably won't. You'll probably be all grown up when I see you next."

"Well, keep writing to me," I wound my arms around her. "And I will write to you every week. And maybe one day we will live together again."

Donny and his family were staying an extra day but he came out to the car to see us off.

"Well, Joan," he said, giving me a hug. "You are sure growing up." He looked at me. "And your hair looks pretty, longer like that."

"Thanks Donny," I said, embracing him. "It was wonderful seeing you. I hope it won't be too long until I get to see you again."

And then Grandpa pulled away from the curb and I turned and waved to Donny, a replica of my Dad, standing there, in all his young manhood, his warm, dark eyes smiling back at me.

I was tired as we left the city and merged onto the highway. The drone of traffic lulled me to sleep. When I woke it was to the simple silence of the countryside. We pulled into our lane and I sighed as I looked at the run-down old farmhouse and the barn, a hive of swallow nests. I felt like I was home.

8

The following afternoon, after I fed and watered the chickens and opened the door to permit them access outside, I felt drawn outside. It was Easter Monday, a school holiday and a lovely spring day.

"It's a lovely day Grandma so I'm heading out for a walk." I laughed, "Don't be surprised if I am not back until late this afternoon. I need to walk off all that food we ate this weekend."

"Ok dear," she said, glancing up from the book she was reading. "Be careful."

The sun was bright and the sky a deep blue. I realized that you could actually see the sky here, different than in the city where it was cluttered with high-rises. I put on an old wool sweater and some gloves and went out into the day. The air was fresh and alive with the twisted song of swallows in pursuit of insects.

I made my way towards Gabriella and Johnny's house. When I reached the creek I found myself staring into the water, contemplating the path my life had taken. I realized that I was slowly waking from the numbness I had known for some years. I had experienced joy in seeing Barb and Donny again and I was feeling a sense of home with Grandma and Grandpa and by this now familiar creek. I whispered a prayer of thanks to God for this return to life.

As I approached the cabin I heard voices and saw Johnny standing over someone who was working on the snow machine. To my amazement I saw it was Josef!

"Joan," he said, rising and wiping his hands with a rag that he took from his pocket. He looked surprised and not sure what to do. But then he took my hand and smiled, "It is so good to see you again."

My heart skipped a beat and I squeezed his hand and looked up at him, "I had no idea you would be here," I said, shakily. "Did they let you come home for Easter?"

"Uh, not really." He paused and looked at his Dad. "Dad, I will finish this later, ok? I want to go for a walk with Joan."

I saw Gabriella looking out the window. She smiled at me and I waved. Sensing that Josef was intent on walking, she motioned for me to go with him.

I somehow knew that we would go to the creek and to the trail that led into the forest. And that we would find that place where we used to meet. We walked in silence until we reached the familiar bend in the creek. Then he motioned for me to sit on a log, now warmed by the sun rather than the fire.

Joanie

"I ran away," he said, taking a seat on a nearby log and sullenly poking away at the old fire pit with a stick. "I just walked out early yesterday morning while everyone was at Mass and I hitchhiked down the road."

I didn't say anything. I just looked at him.

His eyes darkened and he lowered his head. "I know they will come here and make me go back." He paused. "But I – I just couldn't take it anymore."

I had the feeling that he wanted to tell me something, that he had brought me to this quiet, private place to talk to me. And I had a sense that whatever he was going to say was difficult for him. So I bravely asked, "What is it Josef? What are the terrible things that happen there that you haven't told me?"

Josef stood up and turned his back to me. For several moments the only sound was the music of the creek, splashing on its merry way. I waited.

"At night," he said, fumbling for words. "During the nights — not every night but sometimes," his voice trailed off.

"Yes," I said quietly.

"Well," he cleared his throat. "There's this priest that comes into our room late at night." His voice was husky now and he crouched down, still facing away from me. "And he….he," a sob escaped from deep in his throat. "He touches me."

I was dumbfounded. I wasn't expecting this. I'd heard about young girls being molested by evil men. But boys? And by a priest? My heart was racing. My head hurt. I could hardly believe such a thing would happen. But I could see Josef shaking as he sobbed and I went to him. I wound my arms around his back, resting my head against his shoulder. I cradled him, like you would a child. I didn't say anything. I just held him while he sobbed. I didn't know what to say. I just wanted him to know that I was there for him.

We sat in silence for some time, me leaning into him, eyes closed in silent prayer. And then he turned to me, and reached for my hand. He pulled me up and warmly embraced me.

"Thanks for listening," he said. "It felt good to talk about it." He paused. "And to cry, I guess." He blushed and bowed his head, staring into the fire pit.

I still didn't know what to say. I was appalled that this should have happened to him. I had so many questions. Questions about fairness and justice. But I was young then and only beginning to see the world was not such a fair place.

"Do your parents know?" I asked as we began to make our way back along the creek.

"No," he said. "No. They know I hate it there but I didn't tell them about the priest. I don't want them to

Joanie

worry about me too much." And then he went on, his voice shaky, "It was so hard on them when my sister was taken from us. They'll never get over it. Never. Knowing this would only add to their sorrow."

I turned to him and nodded. "But there must be someone at the school who you could talk to, somone who could help you?"

His eyes clouded over. "He already told me that no one would believe me if I said anything." He snickered. "And I thought about it. I saw the hopelessness of the situation. Who would believe a boy's story over a priest's"?

We reached the cabin and he urged me to come in for some tea.

"Come in," he smiled at me. "Mom and Dad will be glad to see you."

Gabriella came over and hugged me warmly. Johnny grinned and waved from the couch.

"I made some bannock," Gabriella motioned us to the table. "And there's tea."

We all sat around the table and Josef was beaming as he spread large amounts of butter and honey on his bannock. His eyes were lighter and I wondered at the relief in unburdening himself to me. I told them about my trip into the city and Gabriella talked about the happy surprise of seeing Josef wander up to the cabin on Good Friday.

"We were just cooking that little rabbit all day long wanting it to be nice and tender for our dinner. I was adding some herbs to the pot and he just walked in the door." 'Um, smells good,' he said. "Well, I nearly fell over. I was so surprised." She looked at him as I could only imagine a mother would look at her son who had been away some time. I envied them this warmth, this sense of family.

As I was preparing to leave a car pulled into the driveway. Josef knew right away who it would be. "I guess they even work on Easter Monday," he said bitterly, opening the door and gesturing that he would be out in a moment. Gabriella rose from the table with tears in her eyes, "Oh Gabaddissh……not yet." She went to him and hugged him for a long time. "Its too soon."

Then Josef went over to his father. "Don't get up dad," he said gently, taking his hand and looking tenderly into his eyes, "I have to go now but I will be back as soon as I can." Johnny looked confused and Gabriella went over to stand by him.

I walked out to the car with Josef. A tall, stern looking man opened the back door of the car and told him to get in. Josef gave me a quick hug as I felt my throat constrict. "I will write to you," I promised, with a husky voice as I watched the car turn out of the driveway and disappear.

Joanie

When I got home that day Grandpa was snoozing on the couch in the parlour while Grandma was preparing dinner. My heart was heavy and my head still hurt. I thought of escaping to the privacy of my room but I suddenly needed to talk about it.

"Grandma," I said, coming into the kitchen where she was working. "Can I talk to you?"

"Of course child." She paused and motioned for me to sit at the table.

"Grandma," I got right to it. "I saw Josef today."

"Who?" she asked, raising her eyebrows.

"Well, I was actually going to visit his Mom and Dad but it turned out he was there too."

"What are you talking about, Joan?" She was confused. "Who did you go and see?"

My head was pounding and I rubbed my forehead and quietly said, "Grandma, I sometimes visit the Indian man I told you about - the one I used to see back in the bush. I really like his wife and…."

I couldn't help it and the tears welled in my eyes. I wished I hadn't started this conversation.

"For lands sake child." Grandma sounded annoyed. "Tell me what's going on."

And so I told her about my visits there and I told her about Josef running away from the residential school and about how his younger sister had died there. "Grandma,"

I said, looking at her as a tear rolled down my cheek. "Terrible things happen there."

"Oh Joan. I don't know what in heaven's name has gotten into you. Terrible things happen where? At the boy's house?"

"No Grandma." I knew I had to say it. I had to somehow clear my head, which was still pounding.

"Terrible things happen at the school. Josef told me about it today. He told me that at night sometimes," I bowed my head so she couldn't see the shame in my eyes, "that, at night, one of the priests comes into his room and — and touches him."

"Nonsense," Grandma's dark eyes flashed in objection. "Now you know that a priest would not do such a thing."

"Grandma," I said earnestly. "I believe him."

"Well, Joan," she said, throwing her hands up in the air. "I told you I didn't want you spending a lot of time with that boy. And now you've even been visiting his family? For goodness sake child, why can't you make friends with one of the girls at school? I told you, those people are different than us."

"I don't like any of the girls at school. They are all stuck-up."

"Well, look at you. Not even 14 years old yet, losing your mom and dad and now hearing about all of this." She looked at me. "What happened to your childhood"? She reached over and put her hand on my shoulder. "I don't know, Joan. I'm not saying that boy is not telling the truth. But it is really hard to believe that such things could happen there." She paused and then said, in a matter of fact way, "Anyway, it is really none of our business. So let's just try to forget about it."

9

Spring progressed in all its glory and I took to curling up in a lawn chair and reading out by the garden in my spare time. I revelled in the warmth of the sun after a long brutal winter. I had persuaded Grandma to let me plant the vegetable garden that year and was thrilled to observe the first sprouts of carrots and green onions appear. On Saturday afternoons I continued gathering kindling wood but we required less with the warmer weather. And then on Sundays I often visited Gabriella and Johnny. I think Grandma suspected where I was going on these Sunday afternoon walks but she never said anything. I appreciated that.

I longed for school to be out and for the summer to come. I wanted to spend more time outside working in the garden and walking in the forest. I studied hard for my exams and my marks turned out well. I would be going into grade 9 in the fall. Mr. Keating congratulated me for my hard work and thanked me for the help I had given him during the school year. And, when Grandma looked at my report card she patted me on the shoulder and said she was proud of me.

"Still," she said. "I am disappointed that you never made a friend at school. Here it is the summer and I'm afraid it will be a lonely one for you, dear."

She had no idea that I in fact enjoyed the time I spent alone, allowing my thoughts and imagination to wander as I sat dreaming in the lawn chair or down by the creek. And that I did have friends, even though she didn't totally approve of them. In the last letter I received from Josef he said he would be coming home on June 28 and suggested we meet by the creek the following day. I could hardly wait.

The 29th of June dawned with the suggestion of a thunderstorm. It was a hot, muggy morning and the sky became increasingly black with storm clouds. "Just my luck," I thought, wondering whether we would be able to meet as planned. Before noon I went outdoors to see flashes of lightening illuminating the sky while thunder roared in the distance. Suddenly torrents of rain fell and even the swallows sought protection in their small mud nests.

Dismayed I went in to help Grandma with lunch preparations. I was disappointed, having so anticipated seeing Josef that day. Grandma must have sensed something was wrong.

"What's is it, Joan?" she asked as we were finishing lunch. "You've hardly eaten anything. Are you not feeling well?"

"No," I looked down at my bowl of soup. "I feel ok Grandma. I guess I'm just a little disappointed because I was hoping to go for a walk this afternoon."

"For goodness sake, girl," she said. "You and your walks. You have all summer to walk."

I didn't feel like talking so excused myself and went up to my room. To my surprise I looked out my window to see a break in the clouds and a brilliant blue sky, the kind that follows a storm, spreading across the horizon. The rain was relenting and the afternoon showed promises of being lovely. I brushed my hair, now long and wavy, and put on a clean, pale blue tee shirt and some navy jeans. Skipping down the stairs I found Grandma reading in the parlour with Grandpa sleeping on the couch beside her. "Well, it turned out nice after all, Grandma. So I guess I will go for a walk."

I don't know whether Grandma suspected anything or not. But she didn't say so if she did. She just looked up from her book and nodded at me.

The day sparkled after the storm. A robin sang triumphantly from the branch of a maple tree. Raindrops clung to the cosmos and there was a sweet smell of new flowers in the air. I glanced at the garden and was pleased to see new sprouts of carrots peeping through the soaked soil. The day was a gift.

I easily sprang over the fence and walked expectantly back the lane, my heart pounding in anticipation of seeing him. Turning onto the path leading to the creek I suddenly thought, "What if he isn't there? What if he couldn't come?" But I soon saw him standing in the creek, pants rolled up, fishing.

"Josef," I called to him, laughing. "Isn't the water cold?"

He quickly wound his line in and jumped out of the creek. A wide grin spread across his face. His eyes were light. He looked happy, at peace. He didn't say anything. He just came over to me and put his arms around me. I could smell him, the sweet musty smell of his skin. He smelt wonderful, somehow like the earth itself.

"Let's make a fire and have some tea," he suggested.

"Ok," I said happily as we both began gathering kindling and preparing a fire on the gravel stones of the creek bed. It was all sweetness and light, that afternoon. We sat and drank tea around the fire. He was like a different person, not the dark young man who confessed abuse to me a few months earlier. But, instead, someone who had a purpose, who had a future.

"I'm finally home," he said, staring into the fire. "And I don't need to worry about going back there for a long time."

"Yes," I smiled, stretching my legs out on the gravel bank.

"And," Josef looked at me and sighed. "He's not coming back. The priest. He is not coming back. Ever."

"Why? What happened?" I asked. "Did someone tell on him? Was he fired?"

"I don't know," Josef shook his head. "There was an announcement after Mass on the last day of school. We were all called to the auditorium and the headmaster stood up in front of everyone and announced that he would not be coming back." He snickered. "If you can believe it, he actually thanked him for all of his hard work."

"That is such good news, Josef," I said in all sincerity. "I am truly happy for your sake."

My heart was full as I sprang over the fence and home that day. But it all soon changed when I found Grandma distressed, wringing her hands and pacing back and forth in the kitchen. "It's your grandfather," she said, tears streaming down her face. "He had a stroke."

My heart stood still.

"Where is he?" I asked. "What happened?"

"Mr. Dawson took him to the hospital. He – he came by earlier to see Grandpa and we found him in the parlour. Part of his face — his eye and the corner of his mouth looked all distorted. Oh Joan, he looked up at me and he couldn't speak. He was paralyzed."

I put my arms around her and hugged her tight. She sobbed, "What are we going to do, Joan? What are we going to do?"

"I'm here Grandma," I said trying to reassure her. "He'll be okay." But I was scared.

Mr. Dawson came back later and took us to the hospital to see Grandpa. When we entered his room he looked up at us and reached out for Grandma. There was a look of terror in his eyes. Grandma pulled a chair up close to his bedside and held his hand tightly, whispering words of encouragement to him. His face was still distorted and he couldn't talk but he could use the rest of his body. He stroked Grandma's arm and some of the fear left his eyes. I had not once during my growing up years witnessed affection between my grandparents believing their relationship to be one of convenience and ritual. However I won't forget that day in the hospital. And the intimacy I witnessed between them.

It was dark when Mr. Dawson dropped us back at the farm. I helped Grandma out of the car while the headlights lit our pathway to the house. I told Grandma to wait at the door while I stumbled around finding matches. Then, lighting a candle I led her into the kitchen.

"Here, Grandma. Sit down here," I said directing her to a chair. She was shivering, now a child herself, and I easily took on the role of caregiver. "I will light a fire and make us some tea."

"Thank you dear," she said, sighing. "I'm so glad you're here."

That night Grandma asked if I would sleep with her.

"I – I have never slept alone," she confessed. "Before your grandfather," her voice was shaky. "Well, there were so many of us growing up and we all shared so few beds."

Grandma had never talked much about her childhood and I was suddenly curious. But it could wait. Tonight I'd leave questions unanswered and ghosts upstairs while I curled up beside her and give her whatever comfort I could.

Grandpa was in the hospital for nearly two weeks but was able to make a near-full recovery. Thankfully there was no brain damage and his face gradually regained its composure but for one eye that remained drooped. However the doctor warned him that he was at risk for a reoccurring stroke, which may have more serious consequences.

Not long after Grandpa came home from the hospital I was working out in the garden and Grandma called me in.

"Joan," she said. "There is something we want to talk to you about."

"Sure," I said, wondering what they wanted as I wiped my soiled hands on a rag I kept in my pocket. I found them in the parlour and they both looked up at me expectantly.

"Sit down dear," Grandma smiled and waited until I was sitting comfortably in one of the old rockers. "Grandpa and I have been talking."

"Yes,?" I looked at each of them expectantly. "Is everything ok?"

"Well," she continued, "I went to Mr. Dawson's the other day to use his phone so I could call your Aunt Alice, and," she hesitated, "well, because of Grandpa's health we feel it is time for us to move into the city."

This was unexpected and a million thoughts raced through my head.

"So dear," she went on. "Aunt Alice said that, now Pearl and Nora have moved out on their own, there is room for you to live with them."

"What?" I was completely taken by surprise. "What about you and Grandpa?"

"Aunt Alice is looking for a small place in the neighbourhood for us to rent. Something we can afford."

I didn't know what to say. I just looked at them, wide-eyed. And then Grandpa, his voice definitely frailer since the stroke said, "We thought you would be happy Joan. You can finally live with Barb again."

But, in all my surprise at this turn of events I kept thinking of one thing. Josef!

10

We had arranged to meet the following day at the bend in the creek. My heart was racing when I found him there. This time he was watching for me and greeted me with a warm smile. He had this peculiar look on his face and opened his arms to me. I went to him and was once again taken by the scent of him. He held me for a moment and then, to my surprise, gently lifted my face and ever so sweetly brushed his lips against mine.

It was a moment I would never forget, the power of that first kiss that completely unraveled me while, at the same time, giving me direction. I blushed and looked at the ground, suddenly feeling awkward and ashamed. What would Grandma say if she knew?

"It's ok, Joan," he said softly, seeing my shame. "We don't have to do that. I – I'm sorry."

"No. Don't be," I said, blushing. "It felt nice. Only......."

He sensed my conflicting emotions and reached for my hand, "Want to go for a walk?"

"Sure." I was grateful for this distraction and my fingers wove easily through his.

He walked ahead of me but didn't let go of my hand. It felt warm and clammy and my head swirled with contrasting emotions. In all of my wildest imaginings I never expected that a kiss would be so profound. Part of me wanted to kiss him again and to see where it led. But part of me longed to be a little girl again without conflicting emotions of guilt and desire.

Later, when we stood beneath the old maple tree I tightened my grip on his hand and gazed at the initials carved into the tree. "Josef," I said awkwardly. "We might be moving."

"What?" he sounded surprised. "Where?"

I looked at him. "To the city. Grandma and Grandpa feel, what with Grandpa's health and all, they can't continue to live here." I hesitated. "But I don't think we will be leaving until the end of the summer."

Josef was silent for a while. His eyes darkened but were warm and kindly. "Well, Joan," he said sighing. "I will be so sorry to see you go. But let's not think about it now. Let's just make the best of this summer."

In some ways it was the summer that I left my girlhood behind, a summer consumed with the passion and longing I had only read about in novels. I lay awake at night dreaming about our last encounter and anticipating the next. We saw one another nearly every afternoon and soon found ourselves exploring the sensuality of touches. Josef never pressured me to go farther than I wanted. But our encounters were not only about the urgency of new found love. We were also children, laughing, playing and teasing one another. We skipped stones in the creek or played hide and seek in the forest. Sometimes we fished for trout and cooked it over smoky fires on the creek bed. Or we gathered medicine plants and made tea or juice or healing salves with them. We embraced those warm days of summer tenaciously.

Grandma never asked me where I was going when I had finished my daily chores and told her I was off for a walk. She likely knew but didn't know what to do about it. And, as the summer progressed, Grandpa became stronger and enjoyed afternoons sitting out by the garden smoking his pipe and evenings listening to his favourite radio program as he nodded off to sleep in the old leather armchair.

Josef often invited me over to their cabin and I loved sitting outside in the warmth of the afternoon sun listening to Gabriella tell stories of her childhood or watching the gentle way in which Josef helped his father skin out rabbits or clean fish. I wished those afternoons would never end and I was touched by the love and sense of family I was privy to there. When Gabriella learned

I would be leaving she began sewing a pair of moccasins for me to take with me.

"These are for you to remember us by," she said as she beaded an exquisite blue forget-me-not on them. "Not only by this flower but also by this rabbit fur I am going to sew on them." She laughed, dangling a strip of soft white fur in front of me. "See. I want you to remember all that rabbit you ate here."

I laughed as well and told her I would never forget her, or Johnny. "Or Josef," I admitted bowing my head and blushing. "But I will write to you," I told her earnestly. "And maybe, maybe one summer I could visit you again." Deep in my heart I knew that might never happen as the farm was up for sale and there was already a young couple serious about buying it. And I realized, as I mentally prepared myself for the change in direction my life was about to take, that it wasn't only Josef and his parents I would miss. It was the creek and the forest and the smell of the earth after a spring rain and the sound of the crickets at night under a full moon. This ancestral farm had claimed me in a way no place had and it was difficult to imagine strangers living there.

Aunt Alice found Grandma and Grandpa a little house to rent in her neighbourhood and the income from the sale of the farm would set them up quite nicely there. Joyce had written to me about a government-subsidized secretarial school she was about to register in, wondering if I would be interested in attending as well. I thought this a decent option for me so asked her to apply on my behalf. And Barb wrote enthusiastically about organizing the room I would be sharing with her. By mid August the couple had secured the income to buy the farm and I began helping Grandma pack up all of the things she wanted to take with her to the little house in the city. So many memories were suddenly packed away in boxes. Grandma had raised her family on this farm and I wondered at the stories that were tucked away in those boxes or else left to haunt the hallways.

One day, I was up in my room packing and Grandma surprised me. I couldn't remember her ever climbing the stairs to my room.

"Well, Joan," she said, looking quite tired. "How are you doing with your things up here?"

She found me sitting on the bed and reading through some of my recent journal entries. I looked up at her smiling, "I'm just packing things from my drawers Grandma." She could see I had been distracted and not accomplished much.

Grandma looked around the room and a light came into her eyes. "Your dad and your Uncle Roy once shared this room," she said and I could imagine her mind wandering back to a time when the house was alive and full of life. "I can tell you. It was never this tidy."

Suddenly she noticed the dream-catcher hanging in the window. She looked surprised and curious at once.

"Joan," she gasped. "Where did you get that?"

I climbed up on the bed and undid the piece of sinew that held it there. "Josef gave it to me," I said, wondering if I should feel any shame in admitting this. "He made it," I said, handing it to her.

She turned it over in her hands and examined it carefully. Then, the strangest thing.

"I know these," she whispered. I looked at her. What did she mean? Did she know Josef's family after all?

"Joan," she sighed and sat beside me on the bed. "There is something I have never told you." She looked so serious. "In fact, I haven't told anyone. Only your Grandpa really knows."

"What, Grandma?"

She was quiet for a few moments and then softly said, "My mother made these." And then she looked at me, wide-eyed. "Her people made them."

"What?" I asked, incredulously. "Grandma, what are you saying?"

Grandma bowed her head, her eyes still transfixed on the dream-catcher. She looked as though she was awakening from a dream herself. A dream of a lifetime lived a long time ago.

"I – I have never really talked about it. You see, after I met your Grandpa, its like I just left that life behind. I moved south, away from my family." She paused. And then, as though determined to tell me everything, she looked up at me. "My mother was Ojibwa. She grew up on the shores of Lake Huron."

I gazed at her, astonished. Why hadn't I asked her about her life long before this, before now when we were leaving? I could have understood things so much better had I known.

"I met your Grandfather at a picnic in Hamilton," she went on to say. "Our family was selling fish at a market there. Your Grandpa's family was selling corn." She smiled, "He swept me off my feet you could say. Thankfully the market lasted two weeks and by then he and I were inseparable. We became engaged and I went home with him. Just like that."

Her eyes had this warm glow and she looked at me with such tenderness. A secret that had been buried for so many years. And then, this peace that comes in finally sharing it with someone.

"We lived with his mom and dad for a year or two while your Grandpa built this house. And then we began a family."

My heart was racing. I didn't know what to say. "But why Grandma? Why didn't you tell anyone about your family?"

She bowed her head. She looked embarrassed, perhaps ashamed. "My mother was an Indian," she whispered. "But my father was from Scotland." She paused. "I don't know why I never talked about it. I guess I just chose to be a Scottish lass."

She was quiet for a moment while I tried to take it all in. A single tear rolled down her cheek. "Joan, it was wrong of me to tell you not to see that boy and his family. And, it was wrong of me to say they were 'different' than us." She bowed her head. "Now you know. They are not so different."

I moved closer to her on the bed and I put my arms around her. Her eyes were moist in remembering it all. "Grandma," I said as I hugged her tight. "Thank you for telling me." I wanted to tell her so many things. About my feelings for Josef and his family and all of the things they had taught me. And about how I felt so at home in the bush. I especially wanted to thank her for sharing this with me because this little thread of heredity brought me a little closer to knowing who I was. But I sensed she understood these things all too well. Perhaps that is why she hadn't asked too many questions when she knew I was spending those afternoons with Josef. Some things could be left unsaid.

11

We packed the old Plymouth with as many boxes as we could fit in the back seat and the trunk. My Uncle Roy would bring his truck up the following week to take the rest of our things to the city. It was the end of August and there had already been an early frost but not before we filled a few burlap bags with small crops of carrots and onions. I stood outside and gazed at the bright sky, savouring the sweet smell from the wood fire in the cook stove. We were leaving the following morning and there was only one more thing to do.

He was waiting, as I knew he would be, at the bend in the creek. When I saw him there I closed my eyes briefly, hoping to remember him just as I saw him then. He'd grown taller over the summer and his dark skin had weathered from the many hours spent outdoors. His coarse black hair had grown longer and was tied back in a ponytail. He looked at me with those familiar black eyes that were already filled with depths of life experience. And then he smiled.

"Joan," he whispered, his voice slightly hoarse. And I went to him and wound my arms around him. I lifted my face and opened my mouth to his, savouring the sweet taste of him. A few tears trickled down my face and I didn't want to let him go.

"I don't want to leave," I gasped. "I will miss you so much, Josef." My heart was in my throat.

He held me tenderly, quietly, for a long time it seemed. A Savannah sparrow sang merrily from high in a pine tree. The creek moved steadily on its way. Everything was the same, yet different. Sadly he said, "I brought you some things." Letting go of me for a moment he opened his familiar old packsack. "Here are the moccasins Mom made for you," he said handing me the lovely slippers. "And I dried this trout for you," he added, blushing. "I didn't know what else I could give you."

And then he suddenly knelt and picked up a stone. A pretty little stone with shades of pink and grey. "Why not take this with you too, to remember this place by? Our meeting place," he said, smiling. "I know I will think of you whenever I come here."

We sat by the creek for a long, long time. I leaned into him, hypnotized by the current and wanting to remember the sensation of my body against his. Finally as the sky reddened in a brilliant sunset I stood to leave.

"I – I don't want to say goodbye," I sighed.

"No," he took my hand gently. "It is not goodbye. My people say it is bad luck to say goodbye. It is, instead, until we see each other again."

I nodded. I liked this. I stood, gazing into his eyes and tracing my fingers around his lips. "Gaabaadish," I whispered. And I turned and left.

A full moon was rising to the east as I walked quickly through the pine forest and into the maple grove. I glanced one last time at the familiar old tree and thought of my mother and father there. My heart was heavy and full and breaking and light at the same time as I climbed over the fence and walked through the field to the farmhouse. I knew I would write to him and that he would write to me. And that I would, hopefully, see him again one day. I also knew that the city would not be my home forever and that someday I would find myself living in a forest or by a river, some place where I could contemplate the world as it turned around me. I looked at the tired old farmhouse, illuminated by the light of the moon. Inside I could see Grandma light a lantern and carry it over to the kitchen window. There were so many things I would miss here but there was also an exciting future looming ahead of me. I would be with Barb again. And I would be entering a new school with Joyce. Smoke curled gently from the chimney and upwards to the sky. The North Star appeared, bright and constant as the light of day faded. I clutched the stone in my pocket and skipped through the yard suddenly anticipating tomorrow.

CPSIA information can be obtained
at www.ICGtesting.com
Printed in the USA
BVHW032014170720
583709BV00006B/155